This book
belongs to

SHANN
on

NOAH

no

A MO

mo

Best Loved
BEDTIME
TALES

Best Loved
BEDTIME
TALES

mustard

This edition published by Mustard 1999

Mustard is an imprint of Parragon

Parragon
Queen Street House
4 Queen Street
Bath BA1 1HE

ISBN 1-84164-115-4

Printed in Great Britain

Designed by Mik Martin
Cover illustration by Terry Rogers

CONTENTS

The Tooth Fairy

Written by Candy Wallace

IT ALL BEGAN when Thomas
Timpson went to tea with his
Grandma. Thomas's Grandma
made very nice teas — well, almost!
She made little squidgy sandwiches
and wibbly-wobbly green jellies and
strawberry milkshakes so frothy
you got pink bubbles on the end of
your nose. And she made rock
cakes. Grandma's rock cakes were
like — um — rocks. If you dropped
one, Grandma's best china shook
and rattled on the sideboard and
her cat, Tibbles, ran in terror to hide
under the sofa.

One day, when Thomas
Timpson went to tea and bit into
one of Grandma's rock cakes, his

wobbly tooth came out and dropped onto his plate with a clink.

"Lucky Thomas!" said Grandma.
"Let me put that tooth in a napkin
for you. You must take it home and
put it under your pillow for the
Tooth Fairy!"

When Grandma disappeared
into the kitchen, Thomas quickly

popped the rest of his rock cake in the plant pot where Grandma's aspidistra grew. That's where he always put his rock cakes.

Thomas wasn't too sure about this Tooth Fairy business, but he was prepared to give it a try. So that night he put his tooth under his pillow and went to sleep.

The next morning, Thomas was amazed to find that his tooth had gone — and there was a shiny new coin lying in its place!

Thomas couldn't understand why anybody would want his old tooth, but he was very glad to have the coin. When he emptied his money-box he discovered there was nearly enough now to buy a new football!

The next week, to his delight, Thomas found that he had another wobbly tooth. He wiggled and jiggled it, but it just wouldn't budge.

"Mum," said Thomas, "please can I go to tea with Grandma?"

Grandma was pleased to see Thomas again. "I've made you some of your favourite rock cakes!" she said.

"What does the Tooth Fairy do with children's teeth, Grandma?" said Thomas, munching on a cheese and cucumber sandwich.

"You'll have to ask the Tooth Fairy," Grandma chuckled and went to get a fresh batch of rock cakes out of the oven.

"Now you tuck into those dear," said Grandma, "while I water my aspidistra. It's not looking at all well nowadays..."

Thomas closed his eyes tight and bit bravely into a cake. Hey, presto! Out came the tooth!

That night, Thomas didn't put the tooth under his pillow but instead decided to take Grandma's advice. He wrote a note which said:

"Dear Tooth Fairy, I do have a tooth for you but it's hidden. Wake me up and I'll tell you where it is. What do you want it for? Love, Thomas."

And he settled down and went to sleep. He was in the middle of a horrible dream where a giant rock cake with big teeth was trying to eat him, when he suddenly woke up. He was amazed to see a tiny creature on his pillow, with miniature spectacles on her nose, reading his note and tutting to herself.

Thomas rubbed his eyes to make sure he wasn't still dreaming.

"Excuse me," he said, "are you the Tooth Fairy?"

"Yes I am, and after tonight I'm going to ask for a transfer to Dingly Dell duty. Dancing round a couple of toadstools is going to be a piece of cake after this job."

"I'll tell you where my tooth is if you tell me what you're going to use it for," said Thomas firmly.

"In my day children kept quiet and did as they were told," said the fairy, looking very cross. She put her spectacles away in a tiny pocket and folded her arms. "All right, it's a deal."

Thomas took his tooth from his bedside drawer and gave it to the fairy.

"But I don't have time to explain," she said. "You'll have to come and see for yourself."

Thomas was thrilled. "Will you whisk me off to Fairyland with a magic wand?" he asked excitedly, remembering the school play. Janice Potts had a wand to go with her fairy costume made out of a stick with a silver star on the end.

"You're a bit behind the times," sniffed the fairy, taking out a tiny remote control that sparkled in the moonlight. She pointed it at Thomas and pressed the button...

"WOW!" Thomas was standing in a vast room that sparkled and shone, as though covered with silvery cobwebs. In the middle of the room was a huge machine with a giant funnel at the top and a moving conveyor belt beneath. At the top of the funnel a big swinging bucket was filling up and emptying its cargo into the funnel. From the other end came a fine, sparkly powder that reflected all the colours of the rainbow. It flowed like a river along the conveyor belt to where it was dropped into little sacks and sealed.

Hundreds of fairies were busy everywhere, scurrying away with the sacks to load them onto little trollies, counting and making notes, bringing more supplies for the funnel. Dozens of little lights flashed on and off.

"See that funnel?" said the Tooth Fairy. "That's where your tooth will go. All the little teeth are dropped into there and what comes out the other end is magic powder. It's the secret ingredient in lots of our spells. We used pearls in the old days, but they're rather difficult to get hold of now."

"So now you use teeth!" exclaimed Thomas.

"Teeth are very valuable to us fairies," said the Tooth Fairy. "That's why we always pay you."

Thomas gazed in amazement at the sparkling scene. Magic powder hung in the air all around. When he looked down at his hand, it glittered in the silvery light.

"I have to take tonight's teeth to the stores," said the Fairy, "and you must go back before morning. But since you're here, I'll grant you three wishes. We had cut wishes down to two, but we've got a special offer on at the moment. Thomas could hardly believe his ears. He closed his eyes and took a deep breath.

"I wish that I could buy my new football ... and I wish that Grandma's rock cakes were light and fluffy ... and I wish that her aspidistra would get better..."

Before he could finish speaking, the fairy factory had vanished. He was lying in his bed with the sun. shining through his window. Feeling under the pillow, he felt a coin! Thomas rushed to his piggy bank and shook out all the money. He counted carefully. Yes! There was enough for the new football!

He took it round to Grandma's the following week when he went for tea. "Very nice, dear," said

Grandma, as she brought in some delicious-smelling rock cakes fresh from the oven. Thomas sank his teeth into one and took a big bite. It was soft and crumbly, and full of big, juicy currants.

"These are great, Grandma!" he said in a mumbly sort of way because his mouth was full.

"Thank you, dear. It's a new recipe. Now you tuck in while I water my aspidistra — it's coming on a treat."

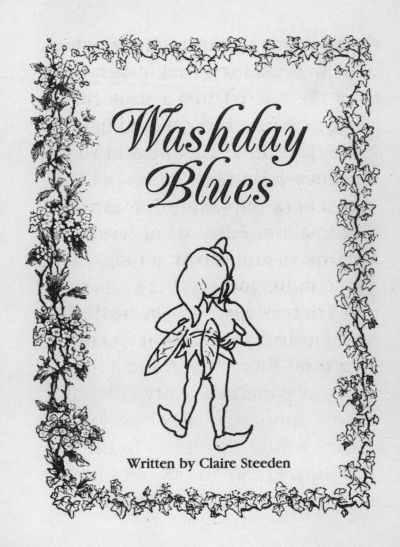

Washday Blues

Written by Claire Steeden

WISHY WASHY the fairy lived and worked in fairyland. He owned a shop called Wishy's Washeteria, which had a little flat above. He spent each day hand-washing fairy wings, which was a very important job as you can imagine. Fairy wings are very expensive and Wishy took great pride in his job.

He was always very busy and today was no exception. At the weekend there was to be a huge party at which the fairy council would announce which lucky fairies would sit on top of the Christmas trees in people's homes at Christmas time. All day long fairies were coming in with sets of wings and asking if they would be ready by Saturday, as they wanted to look their best.

"Oh, I'll never wash all these wings in time," Wishy said to himself. "Each pair takes so long to do. It's Thursday afternoon already."

Wishy lifted a pair of wings gently into the tub, filled with warm water. He picked up a packet

of Fairiel washing powder to sprinkle over the wings, but realized that it was empty.

"Oh, bother. That's all I need. Now what am I going to do? I've got a whole pile of wings to wash and no powder. I'll never have it all done by Saturday."

Wishy remembered seeing an advertisement in the newspaper for washing machines. "Maybe it's time I bought one," he thought. He found the paper and read the advertisement aloud.

"No more wash-day blues. Put a whizz into your wash with a brand new washing machine and let it work while you play!"

"Perfect. That's just what I need." Wishy phoned the company and they sent a fairy round to install one right away.

"Just read the instruction booklet and it will tell you how it works," said the plumber fairy, handing him a big box of powder.

"Thank you. I'll soon get all this washing done now," said Wishy.

After saying goodbye he went to look at his new machine. It was very big and covered in buttons and flashing lights. Wishy sat down and started to read the instructions, but they were far too complicated.

"It'll take me ages to work all of this out. If I just put it on a simple program it should be okay," Wishy said to himself. "Besides, I've got and important evening ahead and I must go and get ready. It's the final of the fairyland quiz competition tonight. If I win I can spend the money on a holiday. I haven't had one for years."

Wishy took all the wings off their hangers, loaded them into the machine, put in some of the new powder and set the machine on what he thought was a low setting. Then off he flew to the quiz, hoping to win the star prize so he could travel to the mountains.

Wishy took his seat just as the contest began. The host asked the contestants lots of questions, and to his surprise, Wishy ended up in the final three, with one tie-breaker question to answer:

"What," asked the fairy host, "is the highest mountain in Fairyland?"

"Mount Sparkle," answered Wishy.

"Correct. You've won the competition and a thousand fairy pieces!"

Everyone cheered, especially Wishy. He could have a holiday at last! He could not believe his luck. A lovely new washing machine and winning the competition all in one day! And to think he had been so miserable this morning.

Arriving home, he took off his wings and was just climbing into bed when he heard an awful rumbling noise coming from downstairs. Pulling on his dressing gown, Wishy went to investigate. The noise seemed to be coming from the laundry. Nervously, he stepped into the dark room.

"Yuk! What's that?" Wishy's feet were covered in something cold and tickly. He turned on the light and looked around. He couldn't believe his eyes. The whole floor was covered in soap suds, which were pouring out of his new machine. He ran to turn it off.

"Oh my goodness! What a

mess. I hope the wings are all right," he said, opening the machine's door.

First of all he pulled out a pair that were enormous. "Oh, no. They've stretched. This pair is ruined. Oh dear!"

He reached in and pulled out another pair which looked the right size, but when he held them up they were full of holes. "Oh dear. They're all torn. I won't be able to mend holes that size," he sighed.

Suds were still oozing out onto the floor as he reached in and pulled out a bundle of wings. As he untangled them he let out a groan. "Ooh, all the colours have run. The new automatic powder I used can't have been right for these wings. The colours have mixed and made the wings patchy. What a disaster!" he cried.

Tears welled up in Wishy's eyes as he pulled out the last pair of wings. They were tiny.

"Oh dear. The water must have got too hot. It's shrunk this pair."

Wishy sat on his little wooden stool and cried, but his tears were

lost amongst the bubbles. "All the wings are ruined and the fairies need them for Saturday. What am I going to do?" he wept.

Wishy spent all night clearing up the soapy mess.

"This will teach me not to be impatient. If I'd washed them by hand I wouldn't be in this mess," he said to himself. "I can't repair the wings, so I'll have to give each customer the money to buy a new pair. I'll have to use the money I won in the competition last night."

Wishy spent all the next day explaining to his customers about the machine and their ruined wings. After handing out money all day he only had twenty fairy pieces left of his prize money.

"At least everyone will have lovely new wings for tomorrow night.I can always go on holiday next year," sighed wishy.

On Saturday morning the plumber fairy came to take the washing machine away again. Wishy decided he would always to do his washing by hand in future.

That night all the fairies gathered at the grand hall to find out who would be chosen to decorate the Christmas trees. Everyone looked magnificent in their sparkly outfits and shiny new wings.

At eight o'clock a list of names was announced and there was much celebrating amongst the fairies. Just as Wishy was about to leave he heard his name being called out, and he turned to face the fairy speaker.

"Wishy, I understand that it is thanks to you that the fairies all have such beautiful new wings this evening," she said. "I hear you had an accident with your new washing machine, and you spent all the prize money you won in the quiz competition buying new wings for everybody. A thousand fairy pieces is a lot of money. I understand you wanted to spend it on a holiday in the mountains," said the fairy.

"Yes, that's right," replied Wishy.

"Well, you have proved what a hard working, kind and honest fairy you are. Your behaviour deserves some kind of reward." The fairy speaker handed Wishy an envelope. "Here's some money that your friends and customers have collected for you. Everyone thinks you deserve a holiday, so you will make it to the mountains after all! Enjoy your trip."

Wishy thanked everybody, and when he got home he thought how lucky he was to have his little shop, such caring friends, and a lovely holiday to look forward to.

Bottom of the Garden

Written by Candy Wallace

DID YOU KNOW there are probably fairies living at the bottom of your garden? It's the perfect place, with lots of tangly weeds, upturned flowerpots and old trees with handy holes in the trunk. And people seldom visit the bottom of their gardens. "I'm going to dig a nice vegetable patch down there this spring," they say, but they never do.

There was once a very old house that had been empty for years, so the entire garden was as wild as a jungle.

The lawn had been neat, short and bright green. Now the grass was so high it waved to you in the breeze and was tangled with wild flowers, nettles and prickly brambles that crept along the ground.

It all looked neglected and unloved to the human eye. But it was full of life — butterflies loved the wild flowers, little dormice

nested in the grass, birds loved all the juicy worms and grubs to be had and, though you couldn't see them, the garden was the home of some other little creatures, too.

Until, that is, the new owners moved in.

One fine morning, a great big van and a red car drew up outside the old house and stopped. Out of the car scrambled a little girl and her parents.

The grown-ups started to move furniture and boxes into the house from the van, while the little girl, whose name was Lucy, decided to explore. It was just about the most exciting thing in the world to move to this lovely old house with its big garden surrounded by a wall. And Dad had promised her a swing! She walked around the side of the house to look at the garden and gasped when she saw the overgrown chaos. She sat down on a crumbling step, put her chin in her hands and tried to imagine it all tidied up with her swing in the corner.

"Excuse me," said a tiny voice. Lucy sat up straight and blinked. That was the trouble with daydreaming, you imagined all kinds of strange things.

"I'm up here," said the little voice again. "On the bird table."

Lucy squinted and rubbed her eyes. There seemed to be a very tiny person with flower petals on her head, sitting on the rickety bird table and swinging her legs.

She looked very like a picture of a fairy in one of Lucy's books. But of course, she couldn't be, because there were no such thing as fairies.

"Are you lot moving in?" said the voice,

"because this is our garden and we don't want it spoiled by people with big boots and spades and lawnmowers and weedkillers..."

Lucy blinked again. "Yes, we are," she replied. "Are you really a fairy? How very exciting! Wait here a minute and I'll fetch my mum and dad — they'll never believe me!"

"No point," said the little fairy. "Grown-ups can't see or hear fairies. Only children. Sorry."

"How can you live here?" asked Lucy. "It's horrible!"

The fairy looked cross.

"Most of us live either in the flowerpots, or the molehills or in the tree trunks or in old birds' nests. They're very cosy — I'm moving into one myself soon."

"Lucy!" called Dad, as he opened the back door and came into the garden. "Don't you worry

about your swing. I'll soon knock
this garden into shape." He beamed
at her. "I'm going to clear the whole
garden and lay a new lawn. I
thought your swing could go over
in that corner." With that he went
back into the house to help the
removal men.

Lucy turned around to see the
fairy sitting on her shoulder,
looking miserable.

"This is terrible," said the fairy.
"This garden has been our home
for years. All our best friends are
here, the butterflies, birds, dormice
and bees. We'll all have to find
somewhere else to live. But
goodness knows where." As Lucy

listened, little fairy figures hopped down from twigs and flowers, clambered out from under toadstools and popped their heads over the top of cracked flowerpots.

"Can you help us?" asked one.

"All the other gardens are spick and span around here. Where will we go?" said another.

Lucy's mother called to her from the house. It was time to sort out her new bedroom.

"I expect I dreamed all this, because I don't believe in fairies," said Lucy. "But if I didn't and you really are fairies and this garden really is your home, I promise I'll think of something to help you. I promise!" And with that she jumped up and ran into the house.

Over the next week or so, everyone worked really hard to clean the house. There was no time to clear the garden. Until one day, when a new garden shed and a shiny new set of gardening tools were delivered.

"I can't wait to start on this garden!" said Dad rubbing his hands with glee. "You'll soon have your swing up, Lucy!" and off he went to look at his new shed.

Lucy felt terrible. She still hadn't thought of a plan to save the fairies! If she didn't come up with something soon, they'd be homeless, and all the other creatures too!

She sat in her bedroom, gazing out at the garden and watching a

fairy collecting cobwebs outside her window. A butterfly fluttered by and settled on the window ledge.

"I know!" cried Lucy suddenly. "I know just what to do!" That evening, Lucy ate her tea with her mum and dad. "Dad," she said, in between mouthfuls of toast. "I've had a lovely idea for the garden."

"Don't talk to me about the garden," said Dad, gloomily. "It's going to take me forever to tidy it. It took me all day just to clear a corner for the shed."

"Well, I've had an idea," replied Lucy. "Why don't we leave the bottom half as a wildlife garden? Then the lovely wild flowers and

all the butterflies and birds and —
er — other little creatures —will
still have a home!"

"That's a nice idea, Lucy," said
Mum. Dad cheered-up immediately.
Only half the work to do! So that's
what they did. When Dad decided

to make a pond in the wildlife garden that summer, only Lucy, sitting on her new swing, could see dozens of tiny creatures diving off the lily pads into the water and rowing tiny apple leaf boats. Little frogs soon moved in and water boatmen and dragonflies, too. In fact, Lucy's wildlife garden teemed with life, some of which the grown-ups would never, ever see.

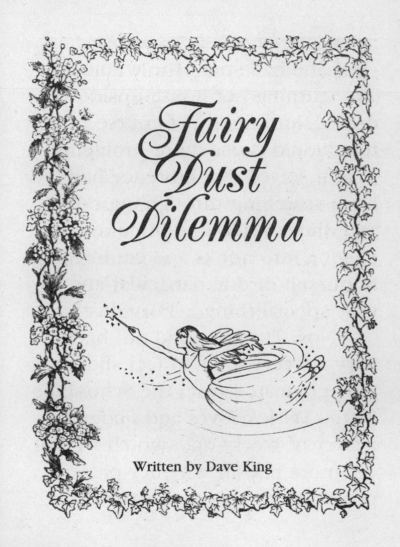

Fairy Dust Dilemma

Written by Dave King

FLORENCE WAS NOT a happy fairy. She had spent the whole day turning her house upside down. Not literally, of course, as that would cause more problems than it solved. No, Florence had been searching through cupboards and drawers, looking in boxes and digging into nooks and crannies. All in pursuit of one particular and very special thing ... fairy dust!

Now Florence had not been a fairy for very long. In fact she had only graduated from the School for Gifted Fairies, Elves and Pixies a matter of weeks ago, which was all the more reason why her present predicament was so embarrassing.

If she was an old fairy, she would perhaps have some excuse for her forgetfulness. But to have forgotten where or how to make fairy dust so soon after graduating . . . well, she would probably never live it down if anyone ever found out. The day had begun well enough. Florence had been flitting around the flower beds of one of the local parks, making sure that all the flowers were tended to (Florence, you see, was a fully qualified Flower Fairy).

Just as she was taking off from a particularly high daffodil — fairies aren't very tall, don't forget — she suddenly felt a very peculiar, tingling sensation. And with that, she fell to the ground, landing in a patch of muddy soil. As a rule, fairies don't like getting muddy and Florence was no exception. In fact, she positively hated it!

Florence sat grumpily in the mud, wondering what could possibly have made her fall. She got up, brushed herself down as best she could and leapt daintily into the air once more ... only to land, splat, face first in the mud!

"Oh bother!" she said (although, with a mouthful of mud it sounded more like "Bob blobber!" which, if you ask me, is a very peculiar thing to say).

For some reason it seemed she was unable to fly, so Florence began to walk home. She looked a fine sight, covered from head to foot with mud. Florence wished she could clean the mud off and, as if in answer to her wishes, it began to rain. It came down gently at first, almost a fine mist, but by the time Florence reached home, it was pouring down in torrents.

Florence walked into her house and plopped down on the stairs, feeling very miserable.

"I'm feeling very miserable!" she stated, to no one in particular. Fairies have a nasty habit of stating the obvious.

Once she had dried herself off and changed her clothes, Florence moved into the kitchen and went over to the bookshelf.

"Now where did I put that book?" she said. "I was only looking at it yesterday, so it can't have gone too far!" The book in question was the Big Book of Fairy Facts, Figures, Spells, Potions and Cookery Tips, a very useful book which no self-respecting fairy would be seen dead without.

"I simply have to find it!" Florence snapped, as she stomped from one room to another. And then she remembered, she had been reading the book whilst

taking a bath! She rushed upstairs
to the bathroom and then remembered something else ... she had
dropped the book into the bath. It
lay on the window ledge. Some of
the pages had stuck together and
the rest had gone quite crinkly, but
she was still able to find the section
she was looking for.

She read through the section

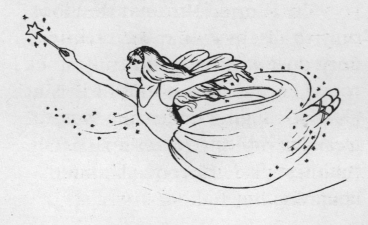

on flight most intently. Eventually, she leapt up. "Ah ha!" she said. "Fairy dust, of course! How could I forget?" Fairy dust was the magic substance which gave fairies the power of flight, amongst other things. "Now then," she said, "all I have to do is find the section on how to make fairy dust! I hope I've got the right ingredients."

She flipped through the book, only to discover that the chapter on fairy dust was well and truly stuck together, and no amount of prising, pulling, tugging or tearing was going to pull the pages apart. "Oh, puddlesticks!" Florence shouted, stamping her feet.

Not having the slightest clue as to what she should do next, Florence stomped back downstairs. "This is stupid!" she thought. "A fairy who can't fly is as much use as . . . as . . . well, as something that is probably pretty useless!"

She began to pace around in little, nervous circles. If anyone were to hear about this, she could find herself barred from the Guild of Fairies. She'd become an outcast in Fairyland, she might even have to go and live amongst the trolls, and we all know how bad that would be!

"Perhaps I can find some fairy dust lying around the house!"

Florence exclaimed. She began to run from room to room, throwing open cupboards, emptying out the contents of drawers onto the floor, climbing on chairs to look in high places and getting down on her hands and knees to look in low places. She looked in the attic and she looked in the cellar, but no matter how hard she looked, she simply could not find what she was looking for. Of course, it might have helped if she could have remembered just what fairy dust looked like. It has to be said that Florence really was a rather forgetful fairy.

Florence burst into tears.

"Waaaaaaaahhh!!" she cried.
Just then, the doorbell went.
Florence looked horrified. She
didn't want anyone to see her like
this, so she tidied herself up and
answered the door.

It was her best friend, Phyllis.
"Hello!" Phyllis said. "And how
are..." was all she managed to say
before Florence grabbed her and
dragged her inside. "Phyllis, I'm so
glad it's you!" Florence gasped. "You
have to help me!"

Phyllis told Florence that she
would be only too glad to help, if
she would only tell her why she
was so upset and why the house
looked like a horde of trolls had

been using it to play a game of five-a-side football.

"You silly banana!" Phyllis replied upon hearing Florence's predicament. "The answer's been under your nose all along!" And with that, she took her friend over to the bookshelf, and wiped her finger along it. "Fairy dust," she said, holding aloft a dust covered finger, "is simply the dust that gathers in the homes of all fairies!"

And so, if you should ever find yourself in a fairy's house, you'll know why the dusting never seems to get done!

Baron Beefburger

Written by Candy Wallace

A VERY LONG TIME AGO in a far off land, lived the evil Baron Beefburger. He had a twirly black moustache and a silly haircut that looked as though someone had put a pudding basin on his head and cut round it. He dressed in black and always had an evil sneer on his face.

The baron lived in a great castle and made his courtiers' lives an absolute misery. Not only was he always grumpy, but there was nothing he liked better than to hurl a custard pie in someone's face. The castle cooks worked day and night cooking the Baron's favourite beefburgers and an endless supply

of custard pies, while the castle laundry worked overtime cleaning all the custardy clothes.

In the castle lived the beautiful Princess Petunia and a knight called Sir Fightalot. Sir Fightalot was madly in love with the princess and she rather liked him too.

But the evil baron wanted the princess for himself. So poor Sir Fightalot received more than his fair share of custard pies and never had a clean suit of armour to wear.

One day, while Sir Fightalot was out jousting, the baron went to see the princess. When she saw him coming she put a box over her head quickly in case he had a custard pie with him.

"Come, come, my dear," said the baron in an oily voice. "I only want to talk to you." The princess took the box off her head and sat down with her chin in her hands looking glum. "What do you want?" she said, sulkily.

"I'm having a little dinner party tomorrow evening…" he said. 'Just for two…" and he put his face close to hers with a horrible smile. "I'd advise you to come, or you might find a custard pie in your bed…"

When Sir Fightalot returned and found out what the baron had been up to, he was hopping mad. Something had to be done. He decided to go and see his wise and tubby friend, Friar Tuckshop.

"We've got to do something about him," said Sir Fightalot to his friend the friar. "He's after the princess and everyone in the castle is sick and tired of being covered in custard."

Friar Tuckshop looked thoughtful. "There's only one creature in the land more powerful than the baron," he said finally. "About 20 leagues away from here lives a dragon in a cave on a hillside. He's the only available monster for miles. What's more, he's not too keen on the baron. I remember a couple of years ago the baron sent the entire army to kill the dragon and make him into an umbrella stand for the Great Hall. They didn't succeed, of course, but it didn't make a very good impression on the dragon. I think he might help us."

The next morning, they set off to find the dragon. Sir Fightalot's knees were knocking the whole way and Friar Tuckshop had to stop every now and then for a restoring snack. After some hours, walking over hill and dale, they arrived at the dragon's cave. It was set halfway up a sheer rock face and they could see the smoke from the dragon's nostrils curling up into the air outside the cave. Sir Fightalot looked at Friar Tuckshop and gulped.

"Are you sure he won't eat us?" he said.

"No, I'm not," Friar Tuckshop replied, "but it's too late to go back now!"

The two intrepid but trembling travellers climbed up to the mouth of the cave and peered in.

"Good afternoon," said the dragon. "Would you care for a cup of tea?"

Now it's a funny thing about dragons. People are very scared of them and run away. When they do go near one it's usually because

they want to kill it and take it back
to impress some princess or other,
which means that dragons get
rather lonely and fed up.

So the dragon was really pleased
to see the nervous, but friendly, Sir
Fightalot and Friar Tuckshop. They
found themselves being entertained
to a pot of tea and a plate of fairy
cakes. Very relieved they hadn't been
eaten after all, they explained (in

between mouthfuls of cake) about the troublesome baron's latest tricks. Together with the dragon (whose name was Humphrey) they devised a clever plan...

That night, the baron sat at one end of his huge dinner table in the Great Hall and poor Princess Petunia sat at the other end looking bored. The baron, with a napkin around his neck, was tucking into a plate of his favourite beefburgers smothered in tomato sauce. A pile of custard pies lay on the table ready for anyone who dared to interrupt his romantic candlelit dinner with the princess.

"Bah!" he spluttered, suddenly.

"These beefburgers are burnt!" He turned in fury to a trembling footman. "Bring the cook to me this minute!" and he threw a custard pie at the poor man as he sped out of the door. Before you could say "knife and fork", the door to the Great Hall opened and in came — Humphrey the dragon! He was wearing a chef's hat and apron and wielding a giant wooden spoon. The baron was somewhat taken aback, but managed to shout:

"These beefburgers are burnt — you're fired!"

"No," replied the dragon. "You're fired," and he breathed on the baron's beefburgers. In seconds they were reduced to smouldering cinders. The princess began to think this wasn't going to be such a bad evening after all. The baron, meanwhile, was speechless with terror and held his napkin over his face.

Into the room came Sir Fightalot and Friar Tuckshop.

"Our friend Humphrey here is going to be the new cook," said Sir Fightalot to the baron. "If you ever pester Princess Petunia again, or throw another custard pie, he'll burn your beefburgers to a cinder. Is that clear?"

Princess Petunia gazed at Sir Fightalot and sighed. What a hero!

The baron spluttered and

choked and went bright red and then deep purple. But he knew that he was beaten. What could a grumpy baron do against a big fire-breathing dragon?

After that, life was a lot easier at the castle.

Occasionally the baron just couldn't resist throwing a custard pie at someone and the dragon would burn his beefburgers that night. That would teach the baron a lesson — for a while, at least!

The princess was so impressed with brave Sir Fightalot that she married him.

Meanwhile, Humphrey the dragon stayed on as the castle cook

and was very happy. He loved cooking and, best of all, he wasn't lonely any more. He never did go back to his cave on the hillside. To thank him for taming the baron, the courtiers gave him a whole tower to himself and the run of the castle kitchen. Everyone agreed he made the best fairy cakes they had ever eaten and his fiery barbecues were the talk of the land. And if the baron fancied a custard pie — he had to make it himself!

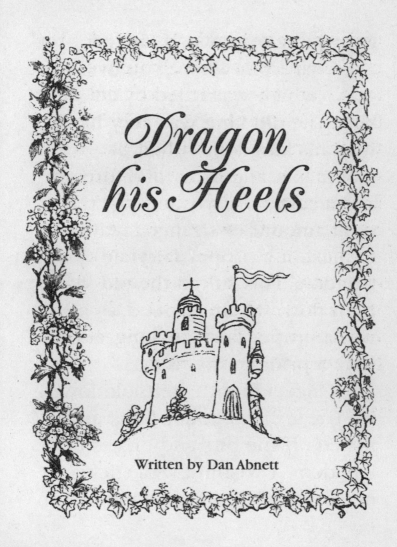

Dragon his Heels

Written by Dan Abnett

THERE ONCE was a land, not too far from where you live, which was ruled by an old king. The old king was very happy with his kingdom. It had mountains, and lakes, and forests, and a castle or two, and just the right amount of strange creatures to make it a proper fairytale kingdom. This suited the old king right down to the ground, as he was a proper fairytale king, and he took a pride in his work.

Once a month, he took down his Great Big Account Book and ticked off the bits and pieces of his kingdom. A wishing well (tick!), a unicorn (tick!), a fountain of youth (tick!), five fairies (tick!), a wicked witch (part time, Tuesdays and Thursdays only … tick!), four fierce lions (tick! tick! tick! tick!), a pack of wolves (tick!), a family of hill giants (tick!), two dragons (tick! and tick!), and a young prince/heir to the throne/son type thing (…er…tick!).

It was a busy time for the old king. Proper fairytale kingdoms don't just run themselves, you know. There was always something to fix. If it wasn't the wicked witch asking for an extra morning off, it was the wishing well wishing it was something else, like a public telephone box for instance. That

had taken some sorting out, I can
tell you. It's all very well getting an
operator who says, "your wish is my
command," but you just try dialling
up a casket of gold, a magic sword
and a beautiful princess after six
o'clock.

Anyway, one particular month,
the old king sat with the Great Big
Account Book across his knobbly
old fairytale knees and noticed
another thing that needed fixing.

"Oh, blow and tish!" said the

old king. "'Tish' is a very rude word in proper fairytale kingdoms, and only old kings are allowed to say it.

Already that morning he'd sorted out the go-slow at Tallboy and Sons Ltd, and helped elect a new leader for the wolf pack (the last one had left to go on a werewolfing course). But when he got to "two dragons" (tick!), he noticed that the account book now read, "three dragons."

He didn't, of course, tick that. Three dragons was far too many for a small fairytale kingdom, even if it was a proper one. Three dragons was excessive. Three dragons was... a dragon too many. It said so in his

How to Rule a Proper Fairytale Kingdom manual.

"We," said the old king, using the royal "we" (something else that only old kings are allowed to do), "will have to do something about this quick smart!"

The old king sent for his son. He was sure he had one of those young prince/heir to the throne/ son type of things. He'd ticked one off himself only the month before. Between you and me, the old king was a little concerned about the young prince. There were certain things a young prince had to do if he wanted to stay in the job, and this young prince hadn't shown signs of doing any of them. "Well, that's about to change," said the old king to himself.

The young prince came when called, and smiled at the old king in a friendly way.

"I want you to seek out a dragon and kill it," said the old king.

"Pardon, Dad?" the young prince said. "I want you to seek out a dragon and kill it," repeated the old king. "We've got far too many, and that's what young princes do. And don't call me 'Dad.' It's undignified. Call me your Highness."

"Okay," said the young prince, a little confused. "About this dragon … why have I got to kill it?"

"We've got too many of them. And it says here in my manual that young princes are supposed to seek out and dispose of any excess dragons. It's part of their job."

So off went the young prince. He wasn't too happy about it. He'd never killed anything in his young and princely life, and he wasn't really sure he wanted to.

But he put on his silver armour, collected his lance and his white charger, and off he went. He looked terrific, just like a young prince should do. Even the wicked witch approved (it was, mind you, her day off).

After a long journey, the young

prince arrived at the place on his map marked 'Here Be Dragons.' He got down from his white charger and walked towards a cave.

"Hello? Dragons? Are you home?" he called into the cave.

"Hold on," said a voice. "I'll be right out."

After a moment, a dragon came out of the cave. It wasn't a very big dragon at all, and the young prince

was quite disappointed (and rather pleased at the same time). The dragon was no taller than the prince, but it was a real dragon. It had a mouthful of long fangs, a tail that ended in a little arrowhead spike, a coat of the most splendid green scales, and a pair of tiny wings. When it spoke, little flames crackled along its forked tongue.

"And you are?" asked the small dragon.

"The young prince," said the young prince.

"Pleased to meet you. I'm the small dragon," said the small dragon. They shook hands, and the small dragon offered the young prince a glass of lemonade., which was thoughtful of him, as the young prince had ridden a fair distance and was thirsty. They sat and sipped their lemonade. The young prince was particularly impressed by the way the small dragon stuck out his littlest claw as he held the glass. A sign of polite breeding, his father would have said.

"So what can I do for you, Young Prince?" asked the small dragon. "I'm afraid my mum and dad, the big dragons, are out at the moment. Princesses to menace, villages to burn with their flaming breath ... you know how it is."

"Well, you see, the thing is ..."

began the young prince. "Actually, I've got to find a dragon and kill it. Dad says I must."

"Oh!" said the small dragon.

"Sorry," said the young prince.

"Must you?" said the small dragon.

"'Fraid so," said the young prince.

"I wouldn't want you to disobey your dad, of course, but is there any way we could skip the actual 'killing a dragon' bit?" asked the small dragon.

"I don't know," said the young prince, thoughtfully. "It depends. Can you play hide and seek?"

When the young prince got

home, the old king had the Great Big Account Book open on his famously knobbly knees.

"Dragons?" he asked, sternly.

"Two," said the young prince.

"Tick! Well done! Young prince/heir to the throne/son type of things who do what they're asked to do?" asked the old king.

"One. Right here," said the young prince.

"Tick!" said the old king happily, ticking.

"You'd better add a new bit to your accounts, though, your Highness," said the young prince after a pause.

"And what would that be?"

asked the old king, starting a new page and reaching for his ruler.

"Friends of the young prince/heir to the throne/son type of thing," said the young prince.

"How many?" asked the old king.

"One," said the prince, smiling.

"Made a friend, did you?" asked the old king, closing the Great Big Account Book and looking up with a smile.

"Yes," said the young prince. "One who's much better at hiding than I am at seeking."

And from that day on, there have been the right number of ticks in the old king's book.

Desmond the Dragon

Written by Amber Hunt

YOUNG DESMOND THE DRAGON was by now absolutely, utterly, and almost nearly sure that he wasn't a dragon. Oh, he was a respectable size, and growing all the time, and he was covered from ears to tail with very tough and very green scales. He had a forked tongue, just like all his friends, and four sets of fine claws as well as a good loud dragon-type roar. Desmond had to admit that he did look a lot like his mum and dad, but, despite all this, Desmond was still worried that he might not be a real dragon.

Each morning he looked in the mirror, twisting around to examine his back and each morning he saw — nothing. Dragons had wings, didn't they? If he was a dragon, where were his wings?

Then, after he had looked in the mirror, Desmond would go outside the cave into the garden and breathe out hard. Nothing. Dragons breathed fire, didn't they? If he was a dragon, where was his fire?

Desmond decided that if he wasn't a dragon, and by now he was almost and very nearly sure he wasn't, then he must be — a dinosaur!

He spent hours gazing at his books on dinosaurs, trying to work out which dinosaur he looked most like, but he always came to the same conclusion — he didn't look like any of them.

Desmond was very confused. His mum and dad didn't seem to notice that he wasn't a dragon, but then perhaps when they asked him to light the fire, they didn't realise that he couldn't just breathe on it the way they did — oh no, he had to light the fire by rubbing two sticks together. And maybe they didn't realise that the reason he left the house very early to go to school was because he couldn't fly there, and it took a long time to walk.

Desmond liked going to dragon

school. He liked his teachers and he had lots of friends, none of whom seemed to notice that he wasn't really a dragon. But then you weren't allowed to fly during school, so perhaps that was why they hadn't realised. The fact that he couldn't breathe fire wasn't a problem either; all dragons, upon

arriving at school, had to drink a gallon of water. This prevented young dragons, who weren't yet properly fire-trained, from accidentally breathing out flames and setting fire to the school. So Desmond's secret was safe, for now.

Then one day Desmond woke up with a fang-ache. At first he wasn't sure what it was. He thought perhaps his head was lying on something sharp, but when he sat up the pain went with him and it followed him out of bed and all the way over to the mirror.

He looked in the mirror and didn't see himself looking back. Well, not the himself he was used to seeing. The dragon, or possibly not dragon, he was looking at, had a huge swelling on the side of its face.

Desmond rushed downstairs to his mum., "Mum," he mumbled, "look at my face. It has gone all lumpy and bumpy."

Desmond's mum looked at his face and, trying not to laugh, said, "Oh dear, I think you have been eating too many chocolate-covered bones. We'd better go and see Morris the Magician. He's a wonderful fangtist, amongst other things." She winked at Desmond's dad, and while Desmond went to get his hat, said to him, "I think it's time to get a couple of other things

sorted out too while we're there, don't you, dear?"

So off they went to see Morris. "It's such a nice day," said Mrs Dragon, with a knowing smile. "I think we'll walk." And they did, much to Desmond's relief. Desmond sat in Morris the Magician's special chair and waited, while his mum talked to Morris outside.

He was trying to be brave and fearless, as he knew a good dragon should be, but his knees kept knocking together at the thought of what Morris might do. Then Morris came in and sat on a stool next to him and asked Desmond to open his mouth wide.

"This won't hurt," he said.

"Uh, huh, uh, huh, mmm," muttered Morris. "Ah yes, yes, I have it, I can see the problem." He smiled at Desmond. "You have a bone caught behind one of your fangs and it's pressing into the gum. The bone is stuck quite fast which is why your fang brush couldn't get it out. You do brush your fangs, don't you, Desmond?" asked Morris, sternly.

"Eth, I oo," said Desmond, which was all he could manage with his mouth open, "Effery hay."

"Good. Now," explained Morris, "I am going to use a little bit of magic, so that when I take the bone out it won't hurt. Then you can go home, and hopefully all your worries will be over." Saying that, he waved his wand, mumbled some magic words, and cast a spell over Desmond.

Some time later, Desmond opened his eyes. Looking around him, he slowly remembered where he was. Pleased to discover the bone gone he breathed a great sigh of relief, and a huge ball of flames came shooting out! Fortunately, he didn't burn anything.

"Look, look," he shouted. "See, I am a dragon. I can breathe fire!" and he beamed at his mum and Morris.

Morris smiled a secret magician's smile and exchanged a knowing look with Mrs Dragon.

"Of course you can," he said. "We always knew you would when the time was right. You can't hurry these things you know. I think you will find that you can unfold your wings now as well."

Desmond looked at Morris mystified. Mrs Dragon thanked the magician and she and Desmond went outside. Then, without thinking, Desmond unfurled his tightly folded wings — they had been there all along. He nearly fell over with surprise. Desmond's mum smiled.

"I think you're ready to try flying now. Perhaps we can practice on the way home."

Excitedly, Desmond waved goodbye to Morris, who, still smiling a secret magician's smile, was watching from his cave window.

Desmond opened his wings and wobbled into the air.

Then, his confidence growing, he soared up into the sky and flew round a few times — looking and feeling like the noble dragon he was.

And finally, he flew home for tea with his mum.

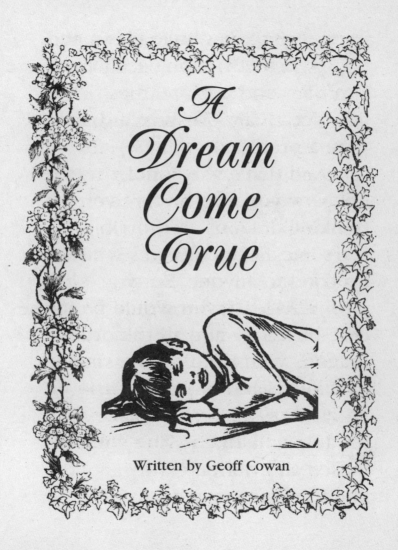

A Dream Come True

Written by Geoff Cowan

WHAT HAS huge claws and teeth, a long scaly body and tail, breathes fire and likes ice-cream? Answer: a dragon with a problem!

And that's why Smoky was fed-up. Now you may be forgiven for thinking dragons are horrible, fearsome, fiery creatures who do no good to anyone. But you'd be wrong. At least, you would be in the case of Smoky and all the other dragons who lived on the small, volcanic island of Dragonia.

It was the perfect place to be; for a dragon, that is. The volcano huffed and puffed gently all day, like the dragons, who were rather a lazy lot. They lay beneath its smouldering slopes, enjoying the warm air and dozing peacefully; until they were hungry. Then they had big helpings of delicious home-made dishes, such as pumpkin pie and fruit flan, all heated in a fiery flash, of course!

Home-made? Yes. Not by the dragons but by the grateful townsfolk of Tastyville, across the water. For longer than anyone could remember, the dragons had been model neighbours. They could always be depended on in times of trouble, which is why the Dragon Gong hung in the town square to be sounded in emergencies. Then the dragons would stir themselves with surprising speed, unfold their leathery wings and fly to Tastyville to offer help faster than you could say, "dragon's breath"!

Whether it was to drive away invaders long ago, or in more recent times, just to fire up the blacksmith's forge on a wet morning, it didn't matter. The dragons would have a go at anything. They were very handy do-gooders to know. In return, the

people of Tastyville fed them with all sorts of tasty treats. Apart from one important exception — ice-cream. The fame of the Tastyville Ice-Cream Factory knew no limits, save the shores of Dragonia. After all, how could such a fire-spouting bunch of dragons possibly eat ice-cold ice-cream? There would be meltdown the moment their burning breath settled on it.

Which is why Smoky dreamt of nothing else; ice-cream was the only food he couldn't have, which made him want it all the more. That and the fact that he was the only dragon ever to have eaten any!

What have dragons and

elephants in common? Answer: long memories. After all, people say that elephants never forget and neither had Smoky. He had hardly hatched from his shell on that distant day when his mum returned from good-deed-doing in Tastyville with a tub of ice-cream for him.

Smoky had been too tiny then to breathe fire. So he'd lapped up the scrummy, fabulous, frozen delight, which now, sadly, he could only dream about.

Then one winter something happened that would make Smoky's dreams come true. It became known as the Coldest Winter. Tastyville shivered beneath the thickest snow anyone had ever known. Everything froze, even the sea in the harbour. So the mayor went to sound the Dragon Gong but couldn't find it under a snowdrift. Luckily, Smoky was practising some stunt-flying nearby. He saw the mayor waving frantically and went to find out what was wrong.

"If the sea-ice doesn't melt, ships won't get through with food for the town," explained the mayor.

"No food for Tastyville means none for us, either," thought Smoky, gloomily. "We've tried dropping rocks on the ice but it won't even crack!" the mayor went on. "You must help us!"

"Stay cool," replied Smoky, blushing as he realised that wasn't the best thing to say. He quickly added, "I mean, don't get steamed up!" He decided that wasn't right either and became quite tongue-tied. But the mayor knew Smoky had something helpful in mind and watched the dragon wing its way back to Dragonia.

"I'll be back!" roared Smoky, through a cloud of scorching flame.

When he returned, he was not alone. The wintry sky was filled with beating wings. Not a single dragon stayed behind on Dragonia. Wrapping up warmly, the excited townsfolk hurried to the harbour to watch in wonder as the fiery flock hovered over the frozen sea.

"If anyone can melt the sea-ice, we're hot favourites!" bellowed Smoky.

Every dragon began to blast the ice with burning breath. So great was the heat that a golden red glow filled the sky. The snow over Tastyville dripped away and the townsfolk bathed in the warmth.

But the ice didn't melt; not at first. It was so thick, it stubbornly withstood the flame-throwing dragons.

"Breathe harder," rasped Smoky, a hot dryness in his throat.

More flames, more roaring, raging fire until, at last, less ice. First, the surface turned to water. Then the rest seemed to give up and melt all of a sudden. The harbour was open at last. Even as the thankful people of Tastyville cheered, a ship sailed closer, bringing much-needed fresh food.

Everyone jumped up and down, and danced and sang for joy. Everyone, that is, except for Smoky. He lay wearily at the harbourside and seemed unable to move.

"What's wrong?" asked the worried mayor. "Are you ill? Do you need a doctor?"

"No, just … ice-cream!"

whispered Smoky, his eyes half-closed.

"Ice-cream?!" gasped the mayor. "But what use is that to a dragon?"

All the same, a big tub of it was

fetched from the factory and placed near Smoky. Everyone waited anxiously as he slowly scooped some up on the tip of his tongue.

"Amazing! It hasn't melted!" cried the mayor. "I don't understand!"

Smoky smiled blissfully as he swallowed the cold, creamy mix. It was the most delicious thing he had ever tasted. Slipping easily down his dry throat, it soothed the soreness from so much fire.

"It's simple," he said quietly. "I am so puffed out, that I'm not breathing hard enough to melt the ice-cream. If I just remember to breathe very gently indeed, I can eat all I want!"

Since then, Smoky has flown to the ice-cream factory once a week for a king-sized cornet or two, and only the odd one ever melts before it reaches his mouth!

So now what has huge claws and teeth, a long scaly body and tail, breathes fire and eats ice-cream? Answer: one very happy dragon!

Wonderwhiskers

Written by Geoff Cowan

DOWN AMONG the plants and shrubs, in many a garden, you may come across a little painted stone figure with a bushy white beard and red, pointed hat. Often as not, he's sitting on a toadstool or fishing with a tiny rod.

These little folk are, of course, garden gnomes. If you've seen one, then you'll know what a real gnome looks like.

Well, Wonderwhiskers was no different, except for his beard. It was the thickest, strongest and longest you could imagine. In fact, it was so long that Wonderwhiskers had to part it down the middle and, with the help of other gnomes, roll

it up into two bundles which he carried on his back.

Any sensible gnome would have cut such a beard and, in the early days, Wonderwhiskers had tried to. But by next day, it had always grown longer than before.

"Amazing!" he'd gasp, as he stared at his beard in the mirror. So he decided he'd just have to live with it.

Besides, Wonderwhiskers was very proud of his beard. It had made him famous! The other gnomes treated him with the greatest respect, and would do anything he asked them. There wasn't a gnome in the land who hadn't invited him home for a slap-up meal. Oh, yes!

Wonderwhiskers was definitely a V.I.G., a Very Important Gnome. But it had not always been like that...

There was a time when Wonderwhiskers had been just your average common-or-garden gnome, by the name of Norman. He had lived in a snug underground home beneath an old storm-struck tree, deep in the heart of the forest. Norman and his gnome neighbours would go in search of tiny treasures to decorate their home, such as shiny pebbles, a lucky four-leaved clover or even a fluffy feather, dropped by one of their bird friends.

That, however, was before
Norman's beard had begun to grow
and grow. Before long it became a bit
of a nuisance. The end would blow
into Norman's face so that he
couldn't see where he was going.
Once, Norman had walked straight
into his friend Tiggletum who
dropped a sackful of forest treasures
on his toe. Even after Norman began
to roll up his beard, it sometimes
came loose and dragged along the
ground, like the time when his
cousin Lightstep tripped on it and
went flying into a puddle.

Yet, every night before he went
to bed, Norman always washed and
brushed his beard before measuring

it to see just how much longer it had grown. Such a big, bushy beard made him feel special.

"The bigger his beard, the bigger Norman's head!" others began to utter with just a teensy-weensy hint of jealousy as word spread of his incredible beard, and visitors came from far and wide to see it.

Then, one day, some unbelievable news caused the gnomes to chatter excitedly.

"King Cracklecorn's coming! Imagine! The King of the Gnomes visiting us!" cried Norman's neighbours.

"He must have heard about my beard, too," said Norman proudly.

"Don't flatter yourself," replied Tiggletum. "He's coming because I wrote to him!"

"You what?!" gasped Norman.

"Didn't I tell you?" continued Tiggletum, looking oh-so-smug. "I found the rarest treasure of all. The king's sure to reward me!"

"What is it, this treasure?" asked Norman.

"It's the place where the rainbow ends," announced Tiggletum. "Every gnome knows it's a magical place, where you'll find a pot of gold!"

"Why didn't you bring the gold back with you?" asked another gnome, called Bizzybonce.

Tiggletum shuffled his feet and looked awkward. "Well, I think I've found the rainbow's end," he explained. "One sunny afternoon last week I went out for a walk, but it began to rain. A rainbow appeared. I saw one end dip towards a clearing. I ran all the way there but, by the time I arrived, the rain had stopped so the rainbow

vanished. But I should be able to find the spot again!"

"I hope so!" frowned Lightfoot. "Fancy inviting the king without being sure!"

It was too late for Tiggletum to start worrying now. Before they knew it the king was on the doorstep and they all set off to find the rainbow's end. By the time they had covered half the forest and walked in circles for a few hours,

everyone was feeling grumpy, especially the king.

To make matters worse, it began to rain. No sun, mind you; just rain, rain and more rain. As they hurried back to their homes, they decided to take the short cut beside the brook. But it had swollen to a fast-flowing stream and that's when the King had an accident. He slipped, fell in and was nearly washed away.

"Someone fetch a rope!" yelled Tiggletum, as King Cracklecorn clung to a piece of driftwood that, for a lucky moment, had jammed between two rocks amid the rapids.

"We don't have a rope! We

don't have anything that can save him!" cried Bizzybonce.

"Oh, yes we have!" replied Norman. He unrolled his beard which he'd kept neatly behind his back as usual. Next moment, he threw the end to the king who managed to grasp it.

"Hold on, your Majesty!" called Norman. Turning to the others, he said, "Hurry! Help me pull him towards us!"

Inch by inch, through the surging water, the King of the Gnomes was pulled closer. Norman closed his eyes, bit his lip and never uttered a sound, although it must have been very painful. After all, imagine how hard his beard was being tugged! Ouch!

But, at last, helping hands lifted the weary king clear and he sat puffing on the riverbank. Soaked but safe, he turned to Norman.

"I hereby name you Wonderwhiskers," he said thankfully, "and grant you the title of S.M.I.G!"

"Second Most Important Gnome," whispered Tiggletum to the others in amazement. "That means only the king is more important than Norman, I mean Wonderwhiskers, now!"

They all thought he had been incredibly brave and clever. As they went to congratulate him, they slipped on his dripping beard, toppled into each other and landed in a happy heap. Everyone laughed, including the king.

And from that day on, the invitations poured through Wonderwhiskers' letterbox. He spent his time enjoying one visit after another, to tell his famous story or show off his fabulous beard. His admiring hosts did everything they could to make such a noble gnome feel comfortable.

As Wonderwhiskers often joked to himself, it was just like home from home ... or gnome from gnome!

Ned the Gnome

Written by Amber Hunt

NED THE GNOME spent the morning sticking his feet into icky sticky mud puddles and breathing deeply the horrible smell that accompanies icky sticky mud. He tried to tell himself he loved the mud and adored the smell, but he didn't, not really ... not even a little bit.

Eventually, feeling quite down in the dumps, Ned went and sat on the top of a little hill, wondering what he was going to do.

"Excuse me," said a voice behind him, "but why don't you smell?"

"What?" said Ned, startled. "Why should I smell?"

"I asked a question first," replied the voice, "and you can't answer a question with a question. It's rude. But then you're a gnome, so I suppose rudeness is all that can be expected from you ... so why don't you smell then?" Ned turned to see a rabbit peeking its head out of a burrow behind him.

"Well, that's the problem," said Ned. "Not that it's any of your business, but I don't like dirt and mud and I hate being rude to people."

"I see," scoffed the rabbit. "A clean, polite gnome. I suppose you expect me to believe that, do you? All gnomes are rude, dirty and smell horrible." The rabbit sniffed loudly. "I don't like gnomes, never have and never shall."

"Oh," said the gnome. "Well, what makes you think rabbits are so perfect, always digging holes for us little folk to fall down?" and so saying, he turned his back on the rabbit.

"Do you really like being clean?" ventured the rabbit, after a while. "Doesn't that make life a bit difficult with the other gnomes?"

"Of course it does," replied Ned. "I've been trying all morning to like mud and enjoy the smell. Yesterday I even practised being

rude, but it's no good," he sighed. "All the other gnomes laugh at me, you know."

The gnome and the rabbit sat for a while side by side, deep in thought.

"Got it," said the rabbit suddenly. "I think I know where there might be some clean gnomes, although I've only seen them from a distance," she admitted, "so I don't know about the politeness bit."

"Really? Where? Please tell me." The gnome jumped up.

"I'll do better than that, I'll show you. Follow me!" And the rabbit hopped off with Ned following closely behind.

Soon they arrived at the top of a steep hill. Climbing down, they came to a house, the sort that humans live in. Surrounding the house was a garden and in the garden was a large pond. Sitting round the pond were several very clean gnomes.

"Ooh, look at them," said Ned in awe. He left the rabbit nibbling plants and flowers in the garden and went to talk to the gnomes.

"Hello, I'm Ned," he said to a gnome who was sitting holding a tiny fishing rod.

"Sshh," hissed the gnome. "We don't talk during the day, we only talk at night." And with that he sat staring ahead, refusing to say another word.

Going back to the rabbit, Ned explained: "They only talk at night, so I think I'll wait and talk to them then."

"Right-oh," said the rabbit, who had taken quite a liking to Ned. "I'll pop back later and see how you're getting on."

Ned found a large bush near the pond. He wriggled into the centre of it, made himself comfortable and fell asleep.

Later, when the stars were out, Ned woke up. Remembering where he was, he crawled excitedly out of the bush and went up to the gnome he'd spoken to earlier.

"Hello," he said. "My name is Ned."

"Sshh," whispered the gnome, "you'll frighten the fish."

"Can I whisper to you?" whispered Ned.

"If you must," replied the gnome.

In hushed tones Ned explained

his problem and said that if they were all nice, clean, polite gnomes, then he would like to join them please. The gnome thought for a while.

"O.K.," he said eventually. "My name's Grunt. Go and sit over there," and he pointed to a space between two other gnomes.

Ned did as he was told.

"Hello," said Ned to the gnome on his left. "My name is Ned. What's yours?"

"Sshh," said the gnome. "We aren't allowed to talk much in case we disturb the fish, or worse still, wake up the humans."

Ned sat quietly for a while,

then, feeling stiff, he got up to stretch his legs.

"Sit still," hissed a voice to his right. "We aren't allowed to move, we might..."

"Disturb the fish," finished Ned. "Yes, I thought as much. Don't you get bored?"

"Of course we don't," whispered the gnome. "We've trained ourselves not to."

Later, the wind started to blow and one of the gnomes fell over, but no one went to help him.

"Why doesn't he get up? Is he hurt?" Ned asked the gnome next to him, in surprise.

"No," came the reply. "He's

made of plastic, as are some of the others. They belong to the humans."

Ned looked round and thought to himself, "I can't tell the difference."

"Do you live like this all the time?" he asked the gnome to his right.

"Of course. It is our job to watch over the fish. We have to protect them."

Ned sat for a while longer. At the far end of the garden he could see that his friend the rabbit had returned. Quietly he left the pond and went over to her.

"I have never been so bored in all my life," he told the rabbit. "My friends might be rude and dirty, and they might smell a bit, but at least they're not boring."

"Time to go home, I think," said the rabbit.

When Ned finally arrived home, everybody made a huge fuss

of him. He'd been greatly missed. He told the other gnomes about his adventures and they were all very upset that he had nearly left them and so it was decided that they should make a pact.

It was agreed that no gnome would mind if Ned was clean, sweet smelling and polite, as long as Ned did not mind that the others were sometimes rude, almost always dirty, or that they smelled a bit. After that Ned was never ever tempted to leave his gnome home again, although he did sometimes go for long walks with his special friend the rabbit.

Gnome Improvements

Written by Claire Steeden

IN A SMALL garden centre, in a town not far from here, lived a gnome called George. At night, when it was dark and everyone had gone home, George and the rest of his gnome friends played on the swings and slides there and even swam in the pond. They all had lots of fun but were careful that nobody saw them move, hurrying back to their positions before it got light.

One morning, George overheard Sam, the owner, talking to Sarah, who worked there part-time.

"The garden gnomes don't seem to be selling well this year. I don't understand it, they've always been so popular," said Sam.

"Maybe they're too expensive. Why don't we put them on sale?" replied Sarah.

"That's a good idea. Could you paint a sign saying 'All gnomes half price'?" asked Sam.

"O.K. I'll do it this afternoon," said Sarah.

George was listening nearby. He felt worried all day, and that night he called a meeting to tell the others what he had overheard.

"That's terrible," cried Grace. "If we all get sold to different people we'll never see each other again."

"I don't want to be sold. I want to stay here with all of you," sobbed Gloria. "What are we going to do?"

asked Gilbert. They all stood there thinking hard.

"We could run away," suggested Gladys.

"But where would we go? We've never been outside the garden centre," said Gerald. "Don't worry," said George. "I think I've got a good idea."

George had watched while Sarah had painted the sale sign. She had used paints and brushes kept in one of the garden sheds.

"Come with me and I'll tell you my plan," said George.

All the gnomes followed George to the shed. "Once we are on sale tomorrow lots of people will want to buy us. They like plain red and white gnomes in their gardens. But if we paint each other in lots of bright colours and patterns we'll look so awful that nobody will want us," explained George.

"That's a brilliant idea," cried Gladys, and all the others agreed. They could hardly wait to get started.

They pulled the shed door open and went inside. George climbed up an old wooden ladder and switched the light on.

One by one they opened the tins of paint. Throughout the night they had great fun painting each other in the brightest colours and most outrageous patterns they could think of. George had an orange hat with purple spots, lime green hair, a red and yellow striped jacket, blue trousers with silver stars and the brightest pair of pink boots you have ever seen! The rest of the gnomes looked just as dreadful. As they stood looking at each other, they started to laugh.

"We look awful," cried Grace.

"Nobody will want us in their garden," chuckled Gloria.

"I think we all look marvellous," said Gladys. "Let's just hope nobody else does!"

It was daylight when they

finished clearing up — nearly time for Sam and Sarah to arrive for work. They just had time to get to their places and stand still before Sam and Sarah walked through the gate.

Sam took one look at the gnomes and let out a shriek.

"Aarghh, what's happened to the gnomes? We'll never sell them looking like that!"

George winked at the others.

"Some kids must have got in last night and mucked about. But look at the colours they've used! Even at half price nobody will buy them," said Sarah. "Come on, let's have a cup of tea."

All day long the customers remarked on how funny the gnomes looked.

"What a sight. I wouldn't have one in my garden if they were giving them away," said one man.

Then just before closing time an old lady came through the gate.

"Oh my," she cried when she saw the gnomes. "How wonderful! I've got a couple of gnomes in my garden but none as splendid as these."

"You mean you like them, madam?" asked Sam.

"Like them? I love them," she replied. "But which one shall I choose?"

On hearing this all the gnomes started to panic. Which one would she buy and take away with her?

"I can't decide," she sighed. "They're all so funny."

"They're half price in our sale, madam," said Sam. "Maybe you'd like more than one."

"What a splendid idea," she

said. "In fact, I'll take them all. I can't do much gardening any more so I haven't got many flowers. These gnomes will add a splash of colour and make the garden look more cheerful."

"All of them? Are you sure?" asked Sam.

"Quite sure. It'll be money well spent," replied the lady. Sam took the lady's address so that they could be delivered. Sarah packed them into a big box and put them into the van.

On the way, George whispered to the others, "I don't want to leave the garden centre, but at least we're all together."

When they arrived Sarah carried the box to the front door and rang the bell.

"Oh good. I was hoping you'd be here before dark. I can't wait to put them in the garden," said the old lady.

Sarah carried them through to the back garden. When she had gone the lady carefully unpacked them one by one.

When they were all unwrapped she said, "My name is Daisy. Welcome to my home. It won't be as lonely now with all of you to talk to. It's just a shame you can't talk back."

Daisy put the gnomes around

her lovely little garden. When she had finished she stood back to look at them. "My you are colourful. You certainly brighten up my garden."

As it was getting dark, Daisy went inside and drew the curtains. After a while the gnomes started to whisper to each other.

"What a pretty garden," said Gilbert.

"There's a pond and a swing,"

said George. "It's probably for her grandchildren."

The other gnomes in the garden introduced themselves, and soon they were all chatting like old friends.

"I think we're going to be very happy living here," said Gladys, smiling.

When Daisy's friends saw the gnomes they wanted some too, so Sarah started to paint the new gnomes at the garden centre. They sold so quickly she could not paint them fast enough. Sam was pleased as business had never been so good, and it was all because of the friendly gnomes who wanted to stay together.

Gnome Sweet Gnome

Written by Dan Abnett

JUST WEST of the snow-capped Candlemass Mountains, at the point where the Great West Road crosses the Green River, you'll find a little pottery business run by a family of gnomes called the Slightlys. These gnomes are kind, generous little people, no taller than a chair leg. They never shout or say rude words or pull hair, they never leave things in a mess and they never have a bad word to say about anyone.

Gnomes are great craftsmen, and the Slightlys are no exception. They have owned the little pottery for years making the finest teapots, bowls, dishes and jugs you'll ever see. Travellers often stop and buy something from the Slightlys' shop. Each item of Gnomeware comes packed in straw in a little wooden box with a label that reads "Slightly Gnome-made".

Mr Slightly is the master potter, and spends all day in the

workshop, making the Gnomeware on his potter's wheel. His sister, Everso Slightly, is in charge of the kiln, where she bakes the soft pottery until it's hard. Mrs Slightly and her daughter, Very, paint lovely patterns on the Gnomeware, and glaze them shiny and bright, and Grandma and Grandpa Slightly run the shop.

Then of course, there's young Od. He's Mr Slightly's son, and a fine young figure of a gnome.

It had always been assumed that Od Slightly would follow in the family footsteps and one day become the master potter himself. Every day, he studied as an apprentice in the workshop. Trouble was, try as he might, Od wasn't very keen on pot-making. He just didn't have his father's patience, or his steady hand. Od's dishes always looked a little wobbly. The handles fell off his jugs, the lids never fitted his bowls, and he was forever getting confused and putting two spouts on his teapots. More than once, he'd lost control of the potter's wheel completely, and sent wet, floppy clay splatting all over the nice clean workshop.

Whenever things went wrong, Od's father would stand with his hands on his hips, shaking his head sadly. Mrs Slightly would say, "There, there, Od," and go and fetch the dustpan and mop.

Very Slightly, who could paint patterns on the Gnomeware every bit as well as her mum, would snigger at her brother in a very superior way.

All day long, Od dreamed fantastic dreams of high adventure and peril. He was Od the Pirate Gnome, Od the Jungle Explorer, Od the Racing Car Driver, Od the Test Pilot. ...He had a stack of old *Ideal Gnome* magazines, which were full of articles about high fliers in the gnome world. Film star gnomes and secret agent gnomes and million pound-transfer footballer gnomes called Gnozza. "One day. . ." he'd say to himself, as he sponged clay-blobs off the workshop wall, ". . .one day I'll pack my things, leave this miserable, boring, clay-filled life and go off to seek my fortune. I'll become Very Famous Gnome Celebrity Od Slightly and send exciting postcards home to mum and dad. Just let Very snigger at me then." As an afterthought, he added to himself, "I'll probably have to change my name, though, if I'm going to be a Very Famous Gnome Celebrity. Something like Brad Slightly or Rock Slightly would sound more cool."

One particular morning, Od's latest edition of *Ideal Gnome* magazine arrived in the post. In the classified section was an advert that quite took Od's breath away.

"Good-looking young gnomes required for ornamental duties. Apply to the Royal Palace of King Barnabus II."

When Mr Slightly got up for work, he couldn't find Od anywhere. He checked the house and the workshop, but Od was nowhere to be found. Then Aunt Everso found a note pinned to the kiln.

"Gone to seek fortune. Have taken clean underwear. Will write soon." It was signed, "Od."

"Oh dear me..." murmured Mrs Slightly.

It took Od three days to reach the palace of King Barnabus II. He was tired and weary by the time he arrived at the gates. If it hadn't been for the lift he'd got for the last ten miles on the back of an ox cart, he was sure he'd never have made it.

The palace was huge, even by gnome standards. Little Od looked around in awe. Big people marched about the place being important. Trumpets blasted out fanfares that made him jump out of his shoes. He had to scurry out of the way of enormous, stomping soldiers, and horses on parade. Even the dwarf

footmen looked down on him.
Eventually he found his way to the
Lord Chamberlain's office and
knocked nervously at the door.

"Come in," boomed a deep
voice from inside. The chamberlain
peered down at him over the top of
his glasses with a scornful sneer,
and dabbed his pen in the inkpot.
"Name?"

"Erm. . . Shane Slightly," said Od,
in a rather shaky voice. He was
trembling so hard that his knees
knocked together.

"Slightly... hmmm," said the
chamberlain, writing it down in a
big book. "And you're here for the
gnome job?"

"The ornamental one, that's right, sir," said Od with a friendly grin. The chamberlain didn't smile back. Od didn't really know what the job was about, but he reckoned that if it was ornamental, it probably meant he was going to be a gnome model. Maybe he'd be paid millions and appear on the cover of glamorous fashion magazines.

"Follow me," said the chamberlain, and led him through the huge palace gardens and down to the lake. He handed Od a small fishing rod.

"Sit there," he said, pointing to a rock on the lake edge, "and pretend to fish."

"Is that all?" asked Od.

"You'll work from sunrise until sunset, unless there's an evening garden party, in which case you work overtime. On no account are you to move, wander about or do anything except look ornamental." The chamberlain stomped off and left Od to it. Od sat down on the

rock, feeling rather uneasy. Two hours later, he still felt uneasy, but now he felt hot and uncomfortable too. He was bored. His neck was stiff, and there was an annoying fly buzzing around his ear. The Chamberlain came back to check on him.

"Very good, but try smiling too," he said.

"What do I do when I've finished this?" asked Od.

"What do you mean, 'finish'," replied the Chamberlain, looking taken aback. "This is what you're paid to do. You're an ornamental garden gnome."

Od was halfway home, trudging along the Great West Road, when he met Grandpa Slightly coming the other way.

"Thought I might find you out here, young Od," said Grandpa. They fell into step, heading back towards the Candlemass Mountains, where the sun was just setting.

"You know, more than anything else, I want to make a big teapot." said Od. "I've really got the urge."

"That's the spirit," said Grandpa.

Od thought a while, then said, "I've decided, Grandpa. Wherever you go, there's really no place like gnome."

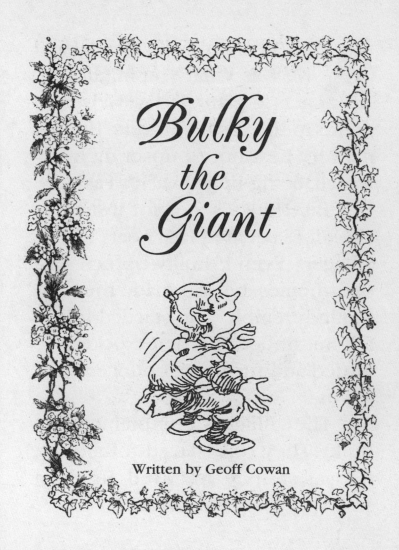

Bulky the Giant

Written by Geoff Cowan

A S GIANTS GO, Bulky was okay. He was what you might call a gentle giant. He was always polite to the local villagers. He did his very best not to upset them, which, being huge, wasn't easy.

Take Bulky's feet, for instance. His shoes seemed like boats to the villagers. Even if Bulky tiptoed past their homes, he still made the ground tremble. The startled folk fell out of bed, kitchen crockery rattled and furniture bounced about.

The villagers complained to Bulky. They only dared to because he was so nice and kind. He even said sorry and promised to creep around more carefully than before.

"I should think so," said the villagers, impatiently.

Then there was his sneezing. Now everyone sneezes from time to time, and giants are no different. But when Bulky sneezed he sent such a blast of air howling across the valley, the villagers had to rush indoors for fear of being blown away!

They complained to Bulky about that as well. The giant promised he would sneeze into his hanky, which, after all, is only the polite thing to do. But sometimes a sneeze came upon him all of a sudden, before he could do anything about it.

One complaint followed another. Eventually the villagers decided life would be much more comfortable without a giant living on their doorstep. So they sent for Spellbound the Wizard and asked him if he could shrink Bulky down to normal human size.

Bulky agreed to the plan at once, proving what a big-hearted giant he was!

"Abracadabra, pots, pans and sink, A wave of my wand will make Bulky shrink!"

As Spellbound chanted the rhyme he gave his wand a few

extra waves for luck. Sometimes, his spells needed it!

All at once, a silvery mist appeared, hiding Bulky from sight. When it cleared, the delighted villagers saw that Bulky was just the same size as them!

For a while everyone lived peacefully. Bulky moved in with a kind family who looked after him very well, and he began to enjoy life at his new size.

Now life's full of little surprises but the surprise that arrived from beyond the mountains surrounding the villagers' valley was big as in giant; the walking, talking type, just like Bulky used to be!

Heavyhand was short-tempered and always wanted to get his own way. The villagers didn't know this at first. But they soon found out. When Heavyhand lay down for snooze in a lush, green meadow, sending sheep scattering, the villagers complained, just as they had to Bulky.

But Heavyhand roared angrily at them and warned that if he wasn't left in peace, he would flatten every home in the village! Then he banged his fist mightily on the ground. The frightened villagers jumped into the air, and scattered in all directions.

"Clear off!" he bellowed. "I like

this valley and I'm here to stay!"
From that day on, Heavyhand
stomped about wherever he
pleased, flattening crops, and
knocking down trees. When he lay
down for a rest, he always slipped
off his boots and used them as a
pillow. He had horribly smelly feet,
and the rotten pong wafted

through the valley, sending
everyone indoors, rushing to shut
their doors and windows. And
when he slept, he snored louder
than thunder. The villagers huddled
in their homes, holding their heads
and wishing Heavyhand would go
away. But he wouldn't.

It wasn't long before they
began to wish something else.

"If only Bulky were still big,
he'd soon see off Heavyhand!"
sighed one.

"It's our own silly fault," agreed
a second.

"We shouldn't have been so
selfish," said a third. "Bulky was
such a thoughtful, kind and good-

tempered giant. He never did anyone any harm!"

"We've learned our lesson. Let's get Bulky the Giant back!" said a third. So Spellbound was sent for again.

"Hm!" he said, stroking his long, grey beard. "I'll have to look up a growing spell. It might take quite a while to get it right!"

"We can't wait," replied Bulky, "Heavyhand is causing too much trouble. I've an idea! Listen carefully..."

As Heavyhand lay snoring in the shade, he felt something tickle his nose. It didn't stop until, snuffling and snorting, he opened his eyes. Now a lot of folk aren't in their best mood when woken suddenly. Heavyhand was definitely in his worst, especially when he saw a little figure laughing at him and waving a feather. It was Bulky.

"I tickled you!" he called cheekily. "Can't catch me!"

Bulky made a funny face and ran off, a split-second before a huge hand snatched at him.

Bulky jumped onto a horse he'd left nearby, and galloped towards the mountains, while a furious Heavyhand reached for his boots. But some of the villagers had tied the laces together and by the time Heavyhand had unknotted them, Bulky had reached the mouth of an enormous cave.

He didn't try to hide, but waited till Heavyhand had seen him before disappearing inside, with Heavyhand in hot pursuit! Bulky had found the cave long ago, during his days as a giant. He knew another way out, if you were small enough. Now, of course, he was! Bulky scrambled out into the fresh air.

The villagers were ready for their part of the plan!

As Bulky rode clear, they pushed against a rock high above the cave mouth, heaving and shoving until they set it rolling down the mountain, loosening others as it went, until an avalanche fell across the front of the cave.

Heavyhand had no time to escape.

"He's trapped inside!" cried the villagers.

But not for long!

How the mountain trembled as Heavyhand raged and cursed, as he began to dig himself out. He worked all day and night. So did

Spellbound, until at last his spell was ready. The wizard's wand whirled and he muttered strange magic words. A dazzling arc of stars appeared around Bulky who began to grow and grow, just as Heavyhand came bursting from the cave.

Imagine his surprise when he saw Bulky standing a good head and broad shoulders above him. Even for a giant, Bulky was big.

"Go and find your own valley. This one's mine!" roared Bulky, raising his voice for the first time in his life.

None of the villagers minded one bit. They were only too pleased to see good old Bulky back to normal. Heavyhand took off nervously across the mountains without looking back.

"We promise never to complain again, Bulky," the thankful villagers told him. "We know we made a big mistake before!"

"More like a giant one!" someone joked and everyone laughed, though Bulky took care not to laugh too loudly!

The Lost Giant

Written by Amber Hunt

THE AIR wobbled a bit, shimmered, swirled and with a 'whoomph' a rather bewildered, twelve-foot giant appeared. He was only a very young giant, and looked rather like any other young boy-except he was slightly larger, of course!

"Oh dear," said the giant, stepping on a bush and flattening it. Turning round he bumped into a tree, which bent over at an alarming angle.

"Hello," said a tiny voice.

"What was that?!" said the giant, startled. He whirled round looking for the voice and knocked the tree right over. "Where am I?"

"Stand still," yelled the small voice. "You're in our farmyard. I suspect you are all my fault!"

"Pardon?" said the giant. "Did you say I'm all your fault?"

"Yes," yelled the small voice,

"Only could you whisper because you are deafening me."

"Of course," apologised the giant and stepping back he trod in the pond and got his socks wet.

"Stand still please, before you demolish the whole farmyard," pleaded the voice.

"Where are you?" asked the giant.

"I'm down here, by the well. Perhaps if you bend down, carefully, you might be able to see me."

And so, carefully, the giant bent down and peered at the well. Standing next to it was a little boy with blond hair and very dirty knees.

"Oh," said the giant. "You're a little boy ... aren't you afraid of me? All the little boys in my story books are afraid of giants."

"No, I'm not afraid," said the little boy.

The giant got down on his hands and knees to get a closer

look. "Gosh, your knees are dirty," he said. "Have you been playing?"

The little boy looked at his knees. "Um, yes, I suppose they are a bit dirty. I lost my magic marble and was crawling around looking for it. This is a farmyard you know, so it gets a bit muddy."

"Oh," breathed the giant. "Have you got a magic marble? I've got one too. Here look," and he fished a marble as big as a doughnut out of his pocket.

"Wow," said the little boy. "That's wonderful. I wish I could find mine." Then a thought crossed his mind. "How old are you?" he asked the giant.

"Seventy," replied the giant.

"Oh," said the little boy, clearly disappointed.

"But I think ten giant years are the same as one of your years, so I suppose I'm about seven in your world."

"I'm seven too!" said the little boy. "That's terrific! You know what, I think my marble magicked you here. I was wishing for someone to play with when the air went wobbly. I was so scared I dropped my marble, which was why I was crawling around in the mud looking for it — and then you appeared. What's your name?" he asked. "Mine's Oliver."

"I'm Bertie," said the giant. "I
was wishing for a friend on my
marble too," and they looked at
each other in awe.

"Wow," they breathed together.
"Weird!"

Just then a voice called from
inside the farmhouse, "Oliver,
Oliver!"

"Oh no," said Oliver, "that's my
mum. You'd better hide quickly."
Oliver looked at his large friend.
Where on earth do you hide a
twelve-foot giant?

"I've got it," he said, "in the
barn. Follow me — very carefully."

Oliver ran across the yard, with
Bertie following — carefully. They

went down past the stables, across the cornfield and into the meadow where the hay barn was.

"Oliver, Oliver, where are you? It's lunchtime." His mum's voice floated across the meadow.

"Quick, help me with this door," panted Oliver. Bertie heaved open the hay barn door and dived inside.

"Good, there's plenty of space. Hide over there in that corner. Well, as best you can, anyway. I have to go and have my lunch," Oliver explained to Bertie, "then I'll come back. Are you hungry?" he added.

Bertie nodded silently, afraid that if he spoke Oliver's mother might hear him. He couldn't stop his tummy rumbling though. It sounded just like thunder.

"I'll try and get you something to eat," Oliver promised and off he went, back to the house for lunch. He gobbled his lunch up as quickly as he could. He could hardly wait to get back to the barn and see his new

friend. As soon as he had finished eating he rushed back to Bertie.

He had brought Bertie a jam sandwich, which he'd hidden in his pocket. Bertie ate it in one bite. He was too polite to tell Oliver that giants make their sandwiches as big as double beds.

"Now," said Oliver, "we have to find my marble and a way to get you back home. You're too big to stay here and Dad said he had some work to do later in the barn — so we'd better hurry."

Bertie and Oliver crept out of the barn and back to the well. They both got down on their hands and knees and started searching for the marble. They searched and searched, but found nothing.

Eventually Bertie said, "I'm thirsty. Is there any water in your well?" He peered over the edge.

"No," said Oliver, "it's been filled in."

"Wait a minute," yelled the giant, causing the ground to shake and the trees to sway dangerously, "I think I've found it! There's something shining in the earth, about three feet down." He reached his long arm into the well, fished around a bit and brought out — the marble!

"Hooray! You've found it!" cried Oliver.

"Wow," gasped Bertie. "It's beautiful."

"Right, back to the barn," said Oliver excitedly. "It's time for some magic!"

Back in the barn Oliver and Bertie sat and rubbed their marbles and tried all the magic words they could think of, but the air didn't move, no 'whoomph' sound happened and Bertie stayed firmly in the barn with Oliver.

"Bertie," said Oliver, "would you like to swap marbles — like best friends do? We might even find a way to visit each other."

Bertie nodded, smiling enthusiastically. "I'd like you to visit me in the land of the giants," he said. In the distance Oliver could hear a tractor. "Oh no," he said. "I think my dad might be coming. We have to think of something, quickly! "

They rubbed the marbles harder and started to invent magic words and all the time the tractor was getting nearer. How would Oliver explain keeping a twelve-foot giant in the barn?

Then Bertie had an idea. "The air went 'whoomph' when I arrived, didn't it? So perhaps if we made the noise backwards it might magic me home."

Oliver and Bertie looked at each other.

"Bye," said Oliver, rubbing his eyes. "See you again?"

"Bye," said Bertie, sniffing. "I'll come back soon."

Oliver and Bertie rubbed their marbles hard, and together they said "Phmoohw." The air wobbled and shimmered a bit and in a flash Bertie was gone.

Outside the tractor noise stopped and a few seconds later Oliver's dad walked into the barn.

"Hello," he said. "What are you doing here? That's a pretty amazing marble," he added, nodding at Oliver's hand.

"Yes it is, isn't it?" Oliver held up the marble, which was as big as a doughnut, for his dad to see. "It's a giant-size one," he said, and smiled secretly to himself.

Bigger, Biggest, Best

Written by Dan Abnett

FORTYODD WAS A GIANT. He was called Fortyodd because he was forty-odd times as tall as a man. His hands were as big as bulldozers and his feet were as big as barges. He was huge. If you spread your arms out wide, it wouldn't be as wide as his smile.

Fortyodd was a gardener. He looked after the Great Forest. He strode through his forest in the way a farmer marches through his cabbage patch, bending over to prune an oak tree here, leaning down to replant a birch tree there.

Fortyodd liked his job. Fortyodd liked the Great Forest. He called it his lawn.

One morning, his friend Fifty-times came round and knocked on the door of his shed. Fortyodd's shed was nine times as large as an aircraft hangar, so the echo of Fiftytimes' knock rolled around the hills and dales for a week or two.

"Morning, Fiftytimes," rumbled

Fortyodd, as he came to the door of his shed, a steaming vat of tea in his hand. "The reservoir's just boiling. Do you fancy a vat of tea?"

"Don't mind if I do," replied Fiftytimes.

Fortyodd washed up another vat in his swimming pool-sized sink. He used a small evergreen tree as a brush. "Sugar?" he asked.

"Two barrows, please," replied Fiftytimes, making himself comfortable on the sofa. It wasn't a sofa, actually. It was a small hill that Fortyodd had dragged into the shed and covered with a circus tent, but they called it a sofa.

Fortyodd scooped two wheel-

barrows of sugar into Fiftytimes' vat
of tea and stirred it with a
lamppost.

"So what can I do for you?"
Fortyodd asked as they settled
down to their vats of tea.

"I thought I had better tell
you," said Fiftytimes, "old Twoscore
is planning to enter his prize
cabbage in the Harvest Show next
week. He's hoping to win the Big
Veg prize."

"I didn't know Twoscore had a
prize cabbage," said Fortyodd, rather
uneasily.

"That's why I thought I'd better
tell you," said Fiftytimes. "I was
passing his garden just yesterday,

and I saw his cabbage patch. It's a handsome crop he's got."

Fortyodd frowned. His brow crinkled so deeply, you could have lost whole flocks of sheep in the wrinkles. You see, every year, his famous pumpkins won the Big Veg rosette at the Harvest Show. There wasn't a giant in the land who grew vegetables that were bigger or better or more beautiful than Fortyodd's pumpkins.

"How are your pumpkins doing this year, anyway?" asked Fiftytimes.

Fortyodd took his friend out into the garden and showed him. There were a dozen splendid pumpkins, each one the size of a hot air balloon.

"Very impressive," said Fiftytimes, "but I have to say, old Twoscore's prize cabbage is bigger than your biggest pumpkin."

Fortyodd was very unhappy. After his friend had gone, he stomped about his garden, grumbling and moaning to himself. The ground shook, and from a mile away it sounded like a serious thunderstorm.

Fortyodd tried to do some weeding to take his mind off it, pulling up some chestnut trees, roots and all. But his heart wasn't in it. He went back to his shed and slammed the door behind him.

Fortyodd knew that he had to do something quickly, or Twoscore would win the prize. Fortyodd was very proud of the row of Big Veg rosettes over his fireplace, and couldn't bear the thought that there wouldn't be a new one to pin up this year. Besides, Big Veg was all he knew. It was his speciality. He hadn't got a particular talent for any of the other prize categories like jam making or tree. arranging.

Big Veg was his thing. He was a Big Veg giant.

Fortyodd took down the gardening book that his grandfather, old Seventysomething, had compiled. It was chock full of splendid tricks and tips. If nothing else, old Seventysomething had been the tallest gardener of his generation.

Fortyodd laid the book open on his desk. The open book was as wide as the wingspan of a jumbo jet.

Fortyodd put on his reading glasses (two telescope lenses from an observatory held in carefully bent scaffolding) and studied the book carefully, slowly turning the rugby pitch-sized pages.

Finally, just as it was getting dark, he found something.

There on page four thousand and one was a recipe for Plant Growth Formula. It seemed his grandfather had got the recipe from a retired witch.

That evening, Fortyodd made up the recipe. It took hours of careful mixing, measuring and stirring. At last, he was sure he had it pretty much right. He poured the formula out of the cement mixer and into a huge pair of furnace bellows. Then, with his lamp in one hand and the bellows in the other, he went out into the dark, to his pumpkin patch nearby. The pumpkins looked huge and golden in the moonlight.

Fortyodd took the bellows and pumped a spray of formula over his prize vegetables. The magic formula twinkled electric green in the

darkness. Satisfied with a job well done, Fortyodd admired his handiwork. Already, the pumpkins looked even more huge and golden. Then Fortyodd went off to bed.

Next morning, Fortyodd's alarm (a church clocktower on the bedside table) woke him at eight, and he was surprised to see that it was still dark. He went to the door and tried to open it, but it wouldn't budge. He went to the window, and found he couldn't see anything outside except a wall of bright orange.

Rather worried, Fortyodd took the door off its hinges and found that the doorway was completely blocked by the biggest pumpkin he had ever seen. It was acres across from side to side. Fortyodd squeezed out of the doorway and climbed up onto the top of the enormous vegetable.

High up on top, it was like standing on an orange mountain, and there were several other orange mountains next to it. The huge pumpkins completely surrounded his garden shed, and seemed in danger of crushing it.

The formula had certainly worked.

Fortyodd wasn't really sure what to do next, but he knew that, one way or another, it would involve a lot of pumpkin-eating.

Everyone thereabouts agreed that Fortyodd's pumpkins were the biggest Big Veg they had ever seen. People flocked from miles around to see them. Families of giants had their photographs taken posing in front of the great pumpkin range. Passing dragons looked down at the pumpkins in astonishment. Dwarf mountaineers climbed them and stuck flags in the top.

Twoscore's prize cabbages won the Big Veg rosette at the Harvest Show, of course. Everyone said it was a shame. Fortyodd's pumpkins were the biggest in the world, but even with his friend Fiftytimes'

help, he couldn't budge them an
inch, let alone take them to the
show! Still, he knew one thing —
his grandfather would have been
proud of him!

Smallest Giant

Written by Dave King

ALBERT THE GIANT had a big problem. Or rather, he had a little problem that was, in fact, a big problem! And if all that sounds a trifle confusing, imagine how poor Albert felt.

Albert's problem was this: he wasn't a very big giant.

Now, if you or I were to look at Albert, we would definitely say he was a big giant. Certainly, if you were to invite him round for tea at your house, you would soon see how big Albert was when he couldn't get in through the front door in fact, he'd probably be taller than your entire house.

But in the Land of the Giants (a

place not too far from the Land of the Pixies and just to the right of Fairyland —you can't miss it because it's well signposted from the motorway) there were some really, really, really tall giants. These were not the kind of giants you would choose to pick a fight with, as you might end up with a sore nose (unless, of course, you happen to be an even taller giant).

So, although Albert was undeniably a giant, in comparison to most of his friends he was a very short giant indeed!

As you can imagine, this led to one or two problems for Albert. Some of the other, taller giants would tease Albert. "Ha!" they would say. "Call yourself a giant — a giant elf maybe! Perhaps you should go and live in the Land of the Pixies, with all the other little people!"

Albert would hang his head in shame. This kind of talk made him feel very sad, and sometimes a big fat tear would roll down his cheek. He wished he could be the same size as all the others and he had tried all sorts of things to make himself grow.

He had even visited a wise old witch in Fairyland, but the spell she gave him just made his nose grow longer and longer, so he'd had to go back and get the spell reversed. But generally speaking, he was a happy giant, and he did his best to keep cheerful about things.

One day, Albert was sitting at home reading a copy of *Gnomes and Gardens* magazine — a publication that delved into the lives and

homes of gnomes, elves, pixies, fairies, sprites and all manner of little, magical people. It was a favourite of Albert's, as reading about people smaller than himself usually made him feel really rather tall. Suddenly, he heard a dreadful commotion coming from outside his house.

He rushed over to the window only to discover that his view was blocked by masses of other giants, out in the street.

He tore open the front door and tried to push his way through the crowd. "Excuse me!" he shouted."What's going on? What are you all looking at?"

But it was no use. The crowd of giants, with their backs to Albert, were cheering too loudly. If you've ever heard one giant shout, you're probably deaf by now! Just imagine how loud a whole crowd of giants can be ... loud enough to knock your next door neighbour's wig off, I'll guarantee!

Whatever was happening in the middle of the street, it was making the giants very excited. Albert didn't want to miss all the fun, so he dropped down onto his hands and knees and began to weave his way between the legs of the crowd. After a while he reached the front of the crowd, and through the tangle of legs he could see a big crowd on the other side of the street, equally excited and equally noisy.

Albert tilted his head to one side and listened. Just above the roar of the crowd he could hear something. It sounded like ... it was ... yes, Albert could definitely hear the sound of a trumpet! He wiggled through the rest of the crowd and stood up. The sight that greeted him as he looked down the street was a grand one. Smiling regally from inside his royal carriage, the King of the Giants was leading a grand parade through the streets of the town. It was the tenth anniversary of the King's coronation, and he was leading the way to an enormous party being held in his honour.

The King was a real sight to see, bedecked in jewels from top to toe and with a gleaming crown. "I bet that cost him a few week's pocket money!" Albert thought, as he stared at the King's finery.

Now it just so happened that for the past few weeks, King Bill the Second had been on a diet. He was rather fond of food, to say the least.

It was nothing for him to eat two chickens, a raspberry trifle, a plate of chips, three doughnuts and a chocolate fudge cake all in one go. And that was just for breakfast!

"You must get some exercise, and lose some weight!" Doctor Harold, the Royal Physician had told him. "And if I might suggest..." the doctor continued, holding up a videotape, "I've just brought out my own exercise tape, Lose Weight the

Harold Way! Only nine pounds,
ninety nine pence to you, Sire!"

Even after the doctor had been
thrown out into the street, the
medical man's words rang true in
the King's ears as he looked down
at his flabby waist. He decided to
go on a diet, cutting down on all
the cakes and sweets that he liked
to munch on during his favourite
television shows, eating more
sensibly and even taking a little, just
a little, mind . . . exercise.

And so it was that just as King
Bill drew near to where Albert was
standing, he gave one of his little
royal waves (which he was frightfully good at), and as he did so, one

of his most beautiful — and horrendously expensive — rings slid off his newly slender finger, landing with a clink in the road and rolling several yards before sliding straight down a drain grating!

"It's disappeared, your Highness." said one of the King's guards, scratching his head and peering down the drain. "We'll never get it out of there!"

The King let out a terrible shriek. "My ring!" he cried. "Oh woe! Truly my ring is lost for ever!" Albert thought the King was overreacting a bit. He watched as the other giants took turns to try and pull the grate up from the drain.

They huffed and they puffed, but try as they might, it just wouldn't budge.

"There will be no more festivities until my ring is found," declared the King.

Albert decided it was time to help out. "Um . . . excuse me, I'm sorry to bother you, your Majesty, but I think I might be able to help!" Albert said politely (he was a particularly polite giant, you see).

King Bill looked down his long, regal nose at Albert. "You?" he said, snootily. "But you're only a little giant! How can you possibly help?"

Without answering, Albert squeezed his small arm through the grate and, after a bit of puffing and grunting (although it might have been a bit of grunting and puffing, you can never be sure in cases like these), he pulled out the King's ring!

The King snatched his ring, and without a word of thanks, waved his carriage on down the street with more than a dash of pomp. This was a very rude thing for the King to do, certainly, but king's are like that sometimes. More importantly, however, all the other giants saw what Albert had done, and lifting him high on their shoulders, cheered louder than ever because Albert had saved the day.

The party lasted all night, and from that day forward no one ever teased Albert about being small again!

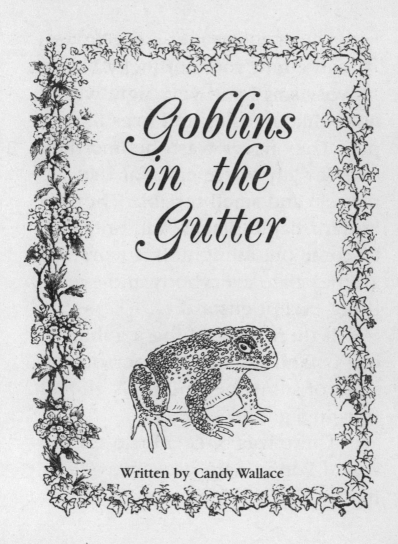

Goblins in the Gutter

Written by Candy Wallace

IF YOU'VE never met a goblin, you can count yourself lucky. They're very small and very ugly, with noses like needles and eyes like pins. They never wash behind their ears (or anywhere else, for that matter) and smell terrible. They live in dark, damp places, and only like to come out at night. But worst of all they hate everybody and everything-except custard.

If there's one thing a goblin can't stand it's a happy person. The sight of someone smiling is enough to ruin a goblin's week.

There was once a little girl called Poppy who was always happy. She had a nice mum and dad

and an older brother called Fred.
Now if you've got an older brother,
you probably think he's a pain in
the neck. But Poppy thought Fred
was the best thing since beefburgers.

"I'm really lucky to have a
brother like him," she would say to
her friends.

Poppy thought school was
absolutely brilliant, too. There was
nothing she liked more than two
pages of sums to do — unless it
was three pages of sums. Everybody
else thought Miss Crochet the
teacher was horrible and grumpy
and made them work too hard.
They put chewing gum on her

chair and daddy-long-legs in her desk to make her screech. But Poppy thought she was funny and laughed at her.

Outside Poppy's house there was a drain in the road. If you looked down it all you could see was dirty water at the bottom. It was dark and smelly and full of old

lolly sticks, dead leaves and spiders.
There were goblins living in that
drain. You couldn't see them, but if
you knelt down and put your ear to
the ground you might have heard
them arguing. Goblins are always
arguing and fighting.

They had moved there when
Chestnut Tree Close was dug up to
lay new water pipes. They hadn't
minded the noisy road drills. But
laughing workmen who sang loud
songs and told jokes were more
than a goblin could stomach. So, at
dead of night, they had packed up
and made their way to Acacia
Avenue, and the drain outside
Poppy's house.

They soon realised this was a big mistake.

"It makes me feel sick," said Gruel, the oldest, grumpiest goblin, "every time I see Whatshername skipping along to school with a big smile on her face. She should be arrested for humming without due care and attention."

"Well, I think we should sort her out," said a fat goblin called Squelch, who thought all children should be made into savoury pies. "If we can't wipe that smile off her face, I'm a pixie."

The next morning, two goblins popped their heads through the grille of the drain. Their mean little eyes darted about to make sure no one was around. They jumped out holding a length of dirty old string, tied one end to the drain and tiptoed across the pavement to tie the other end to the hedge outside Poppy's house.

"There's nothing like a couple of grazed knees to make children cry!" sniggered one. "Let's hope she

enjoys the trip!" giggled the other and they jumped back inside the drain to wait and listen.

Sure enough, a few minutes later there was a cry and a commotion. Gleefully the goblins peeped out to survey their handiwork. But it wasn't Poppy they saw on the pavement — it was an old man, sitting with arms and legs waving in the air!

"Oh dear, oh dear!" said the old man. "Whatever happened? Thank goodness nothing's broken. I could have had a nasty fall!"

Poppy's mum and dad rushed out of the house to help him. So did Mr Entwhistle from across the road and Mrs Ramsbottom from number 67 .

"Are you all right, dear?" asked Poppy's mum, who was very worried about the old man. "Come on in and have a nice cup of tea. What horrid children would tie string across the path like that! Just wait till I catch them!"

"When you've had a nice cuppa I'll take you home," said Mrs Ramsbottom, anxiously.

"Thank you so much!" replied the old man, as they helped him out of the hedge. "Do you know, I've lived in this street for two years and no one has ever spoken to me before!" They all went into

Poppy's house. "Well you can come round for tea any time, Mr — er —."

"Brown. Ernest Brown," said the old man, and smiled to himself happily.

"Rats!" hissed Spodworthy, Goblin-in-Chief, to Gruel. "We got the wrong person! We'd better get it right next time! All we've done is make someone else happy too!"

That night, Squelch crept along the drains underground, up the pipes and through the plughole into the kitchen sink in Poppy's house. There on the table was her lunchbox for school, which Poppy's mum always packed the night before. He scurried to the rubbish

bin and picked out a horrible
smelly half-eaten fish. Then he
opened her lunch box, took out all
the cheese from the sandwiches

and put the fish in instead! He threw the cheese in the bin, and put the chocolate cake in his pocket for later!

"If that doesn't make her cry at school today, I don't know what will!" he smirked, and dived back down the plughole. Squelch couldn't think of anything worse than going without your lunch...

Poppy was none the wiser. In the morning she walked out of the garden gate holding her lunchbox and humming a tune.

Before long, she noticed a little cat following her, jumping up at the lunchbox and swiping it with her paw.

"Hello, pussycat!" said Poppy, bending down to stroke her. "Oh dear, you look very thin and your fur is all matted and dull. Haven't you got a home?"

The little cat gave a feeble miaow and sniffed and pawed at Poppy's lunchbox.

"You can have a sandwich if you like," said Poppy, and opened up her box. When she saw the fish sandwiches, she laughed. "Poor Mum must have been a bit muddled last night!" she said. "Come on, pussycat. Fred's always wanted a cat and you need someone to look after you."

Poppy picked up the cat and

took her home. Fred was thrilled. The goblins watched as Fred and Poppy fed the cat and played with her in the front garden. Spodworthy was beside himself with fury.

"Fools! Imbeciles! You've managed to turn one happy child and one miserable cat into two horribly happy children and one disgustingly happy cat!" he screamed at the other goblins.

That night, the goblins held a special committee meeting. They argued and shouted and jumped up and down. They boxed each others ears. Spodworthy stamped on Squelch's foot. Finally they came to a decision.

In the morning, Poppy kissed the cat (newly named Tiddles) goodbye and waved to Mr Brown. She skipped along the pavement, past the dark, silent drain.

The goblins had gone.

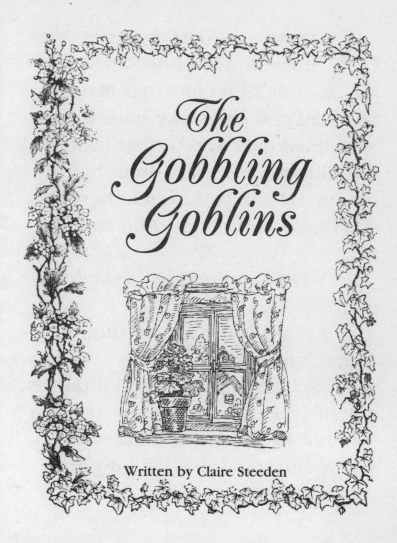

The Gobbling Goblins

Written by Claire Steeden

AMY WAS FAST ASLEEP and dreaming of chocolate cake. At eight o'clock her alarm went off and she woke with a start. She rolled over and turned it off. As she did so she felt a pain in her tummy. "Ouch. Mum, come here," she called. Her mum came running in.

"What's the matter?" asked her mum.

"I don't feel well. My tummy aches," said Amy.

"Well, stay in bed and I'll put on one of your story tapes and you can listen to it while I do some work," said Mum. Amy snuggled into her duvet listening to a story about goblins, and gazing at the doll's house in the corner of her room. After a while she felt sleepy, but as she began to doze she thought she saw two little faces looking out through her doll's house window. She woke again later, when her mum came into the room. "How are you feeling?" asked Mum.

"I still feel a bit poorly. I just had a funny dream about goblins living in my doll's house," said Amy.

"There aren't any goblins in your doll's house, silly," laughed Mum.

"I wish there were. It would be fun," said Amy.

"No it wouldn't. Goblins are

usually very naughty," said Mum. "Are you hungry? Would you like some lunch?"

"Not really," mumbled Amy.

"Well, how about a nice boiled egg with soldiers?" suggested Mum.

Amy followed her mum downstairs and lay on the sofa watching television while mum made lunch.

"Eat up," said Mum, as she set down a tray in front of Amy.

"But I don't feel very hungry," whined Amy.

"How about if I help you?" asked Mum, and she dipped the spoon into the egg. "O.K.," smiled Amy.

Just as the spoon got close to Amy's mouth, the phone rang and her mum turned away to answer it. Amy was about to eat the egg when two goblins ran out from behind the salt and pepper pots, jumped up and ate all the egg off the spoon. Amy could not believe her eyes! They looked just like the goblins in her dream. They ran back to their hiding place, giggling.

Amy's mum put the phone

down, turned back to Amy and looked at the spoon.

"So you are hungry after all," said Mum.

"I didn't eat it. It was the goblins hiding behind the pepper pot," said Amy, pointing to the tray. "Didn't you see them?"

"No," said Mum. "You and your goblins. Let's get on with lunch.

"But I'm not hungry," said Amy.

"Well, you soon gobbled the last spoonful. I know, if I look away

maybe the goblins will eat it again," laughed Mum. She was happy to play Amy's game if it meant she ate her lunch. So she dipped a soldier into the egg, held it in front of Amy, and looked away.

Amy sat and stared in amazement as again the goblins dashed out, ate the food and ran back.

Amy started to giggle because they looked so funny. Mum turned back and saw that the soldier had gone.

"Who could have eaten that?" asked Mum with a smile.

"The goblins ate it," laughed Amy.

"They must be hungry. Let's give them some more," said Mum. Amy and her mum sat on the sofa playing this game while the goblins ran back and forth eating Amy's lunch, until it was all gone. "That was fun," said Amy.

"Good," said Mum. "Lie here and watch television, and you'll soon start to feel better now you've eaten." As Mum left the room the goblins crept out and called to Amy. "Psstt, thanks for lunch."

"That's all right. I wasn't hungry. Where did you come from?" asked Amy.

"Oh, we live in a lovely little house upstairs," replied the goblins.

"What! In my doll's house? So it was your faces I saw at the window!" said Amy.

"Who are you talking to?" asked Mum, coming back into the room. "The goblins," answered Amy. "Look!" She pointed to where the goblins had been, but they had dived behind a cushion when they heard Mum coming.

"I think you've been dreaming again," said Mum.

Amy lay on the sofa watching T.V., but after a while she felt hungry, and asked her mum for something to eat.

"You can't feel hungry after eating all that lunch," said Mum

"But I didn't eat any lunch. The goblins did," whined Amy.

"Don't be silly. That was only a game."

"But they did eat it. They came downstairs from my doll's house," Amy explained.

"You've been having lots of funny dreams this morning while you've been poorly. There are no such things as goblins," laughed Mum.

"There are. They're real. I saw them. And they ate my lunch and now I'm hungry," said Amy.

Munch whispered something to Crunch and they jumped down onto the floor and dashed into the doll's house. Amy sat and waited, but not for long. Soon Munch and Crunch came running out with trays filled with all the plastic food from the doll's house kitchen. "I can't eat that," laughed Amy, "it's not real."

"Of course you can eat it," said Munch. "Watch."

With that Munch and Crunch held hands and started jumping up and down.

As they did so they called out, "Plastic food, you look so yummy.

Become real, to fill my tummy!"

With that there was a bright flash, and when Amy opened her

eyes there in front of her was a real feast! "Oh, wow," she cried. "Thank you."

Amy tucked into sandwiches, cakes, crisps, sausage rolls, biscuits and ice cream.

After a while she said, "I'm full. I can't eat any more. Thank you."

"We'd better clear up before your mum comes," said Crunch. With another flash all the food vanished.

"We'd better go. Sorry you got into trouble, but I hope you enjoyed our lunch," said Crunch.

"Oh, I did. It was much nicer than a boiled egg," said Amy and they all laughed. They said goodbye and in a flash the goblins had gone.

Amy was just licking the last bit of ice cream from her lips when Mum came in with a tray of food.

"I thought that you might want some tea and biscuits," said Mum.

"Yes, please," said Amy.

Mum sat on the bed and gave Amy the tray. Just then the phone rang and Mum went to answer it. When she came back all the biscuits had gone.

"Who ate all those?" asked Mum.

"I did," replied Amy. "The goblins have gone home."

The Good Goblin

Written by Candy Wallace

DEEP IN THE HEART of a great
forest, a long way away and
a long time ago, lived a gang
of goblins. Most of them were just
like goblins everywhere —
horrible.

Small goblins attended school
to learn how to be nasty. Soon they
were taking exams in Telling Lies,
Cheating, General Nastiness 1 and
2, Sneering and Loathing. The
goblins who were better at doing
things with their hands took
Pinching, Punching and Stealing
Things. If a goblin passed all his
exams he got a Certificate in
Nastiness and became a fully
qualified goblin.

One of them, however, didn't quite fit in. His name was Pookie and he never managed to pass a single exam. When Question 1 said, "Describe, in not more than one hundred words, how you would steal a little girl's birthday cake," he wrote, "Well, actually I wouldn't do that because it's not really an awfully nice thing to do."

Question 4 said, "How would you make someone feel really miserable? Would you a. laugh at their skinny legs, b. trip them up, or c. give them a cuddle?" Pookie wrote, "Give them a cuddle," and got nought out of twenty.

The goblins used to go out on

stealing expeditions. You know the sort of thing, making off with one sock so someone spends the next week trying to find it and ends up

with not one matching pair. Or sneaking into a little boy's bedroom and taking his favourite toy.

All the other goblins had given up on Pookie. They left him behind on these outings because as fast as they were stealing things, Pookie was taking them back. Once they returned and found he'd washed all their nicely grimy clothes and put them out to dry in the sunshine. He was absolutely impossible.

They tried taking him to the goblin doctor. "Can you give Pookie some medicine to make him nastier?" they asked.

"Well, young goblin," said the doctor to Pookie gravely, "I'm afraid this medicine is going to taste nice, but unless a medicine tastes nice, it won't do you any good at all. You'll have to be brave and take it every day."

Pookie said the doctor was very kind and promised to follow his instructions

A week later the goblins went to visit Pookie to see if he had become any nastier.

"We're off to rip holes in shopping bags so all the food falls out!" they said to him, temptingly. "You'll enjoy that won't you, Pookie?"

"It's very good of you to invite me," replied Pookie, "but I promised a blackbird I'd help her make her nest today. I'm most frightfully sorry." And off he went, whistling a happy tune.

Nothing seemed to work. It was time to try something drastic.

"We'll go and ask the wizard to sort him out!" they cried.

"He's the only one who can make Pookie nasty!"

Sure enough, in a cave near the forest lived an old wizard called Woozle. Woozle had a terrible temper and usually threw things at the goblins when they came near. But many's the time the goblins had seen him chanting and mixing strange potions. They saw him turn a snail into a teapot and a.rabbit into a toothbrush. Changing a nice goblin into a nasty goblin should be a piece of cake for a clever wizard like him.

This was certainly a challenge for a wizard of genius and creative brilliance such as himself.

What the goblins didn't know was that Woozle wasn't very good at casting spells and was always getting into trouble. There was that embarrassing episode when he'd turned his Uncle Tertius into a pig, not to mention the unfortunate incident when he tried to magic his donkey into a horse. The next thing he knew there was a one-hundred-

and-sixty-pound centipede tied up outside his cave.

He was wrestling with a spell to make acorns into cupcakes when the goblins approached him, nervously, one morning. Luckily for the goblins the wizard was in a good mood. He;d managed to turn his budgie into a chocolate chip cookie, so he felt he was on the right track.

"We need your help," they said, and explained about Pookie. "He's a very bad influence on the younger goblins," they told him. "There must be something you can do." The wizard looked thoughtful.

"All right, I'll do it," said Woozle.

"I'll come over tomorrow with one of my magic potions. I'm sure it will be the simplest of matters to transform this poor, deluded young goblin into a fine, unpleasant young goblin. Leave it to me!"

The next day, all the goblins gathered together in a clearing to wait for the wizard's arrival. Pookie strolled along too, curious as to why everyone was so excited. Then he noticed they were all sniggering and pointing at him and he began to feel rather uncomfortable.

At last, the wizard arrived on foot. He was going to come on his centipede, but had changed his mind. It was a very obliging centipede and much better tempered than the donkey had been, but Woozle felt rather seasick whenever he tried to ride on him. It must have been all those legs.

So, when he arrived, the wizard was rather tired. He sat down on a rock puffing and blowing and coughing.

"I've ... brought ... the ... potion," he wheezed and wiped his brow. Reaching into his pocket he took out a little bottle with bright yellow liquid in it. "Where is the goblin in question?"

Instantly, Pookie knew it was him. He found himself pushed forwards by the other goblins. The wizard drew a chalk circle around Pookie and asked all the other goblins to stand around him and hold hands. Then he sprinkled the yellow mixture around the chalk circle.

Woozle took out a pair of wire spectacles and balanced them on his nose. Then he pulled out a tattered piece of paper covered in

scribbles.

"Er, yes now, here it is, er, ah yes, here is nice where should be nasty, change this situation fasty!" The wizard took his specs off and coughed nervously. "Poetry was never my strong point," he apologised.

Nevertheless, he felt pleased. He looked at Pookie hopefully for signs of a sneer. But Pookie wasn't looking at him. Pookie was looking at all the other goblins. They were dancing towards the wizard, hand-in-hand.

"Thanks most awfully for coming to see us!" said one. "Have a nice cup of tea before you go," cried another.

"Do forgive us," said the Chief Goblin. "I'm afraid we can't stay, we simply must dash and help some old ladies cross the road. Good morning to you!"

The goblins skipped off happily down the path, pausing only to pick daisies and wave at passing butterflies.

Pookie and the wizard were left, staring in astonishment. They looked at each other and gulped.

"That was a very good spell, Mr Wizard," said Pookie at last. "You must be the cleverest wizard in the whole world."

Woozle put his spectacles

away. He thought it was a good spell to finish his wizard career. It was time to take up gardening.

A Nasty Case of Goblins

Written by Dan Abnett

LORD DUBLOON of Steep Castle took a step back in amazement. "I've g...got wh..what?" he stammered.

The dwarf from the Council straightened the front of his overalls and tucked his stubby pencil behind his stubby ear. "You've got the worst case of goblins I've seen in all my long years."

Lord Dubloon's legs suddenly decided he needed to sit down, and he staggered backwards onto his huge chair. "Goblins?" he asked. "In my castle?"

The dwarf nodded and shrugged. "No doubt about it, your

Lordship. You have got what we in the pest control business call an infestation. They're everywhere."

Lord Dubloon sagged. "This is terrible. The neighbours will talk. I'm a respectable lord, I've got responsibilities. I have to wear a robe and medals and give orders and have banquets and ... and things. I can't have the family castle overrun with goblins." He said the word like it was the rudest one he'd ever heard.

He got to his feet. "Are you quite sure?" he asked, hoping it was all a joke.

The dwarf nodded, pointing to a stretch of skirting board between two suits of armour. "Look," he said. "That hole. .."

"Mice!" said Lord Dubloon quickly.

"Mice don't need a hole a foot high, your Lordship," said the dwarf. "Listen..." He knelt down and rapped hard on the wooden skirting. Lord Dubloon leaned over to hear.

The unmistakable sound of cackling laughter floated up out of the hole. Goblins, sniggering.

The dwarf looked up at Lord Dubloon. "Goblins," he stated, somewhat shortly.

Lord Dubloon sighed and thought for a while. "Can you do anything about them?" he asked.

The dwarf frowned and whistled through his teeth. "No," he said, at last. "But," he added, "I know a dwarf who can."

A second dwarf arrived at Steep Castle the next morning, pushing a handcart with a sign painted on the side. The sign read:

"Short Brothers, Pest Control. Biggest in the business. Gorgons, Goblins and Cockroaches a speciality." Lord Dubloon hurried outside. "Lord Dubloon! A pleasure!" said Mr Short smartly. "They tell me it's goblins you've got."

Lord Dubloon nodded.

"Right ho!" said the dwarf. He

put on a pair of big leather gloves, a pair of rubber waders, a welding mask and goggles, and a hard hat with a miner's lamp attached to it.

"Mmmgg mghhmmp ggmmgp hhgg," he said.

"Pardon?" asked Lord Dubloon.

Mr Short raised the visor of his welding mask. "Show me the way!" he repeated. "And could you give me a hand with my equipment?"

Weighed down with ropes and ladders and sink plungers and butterfly nets, Lord Dubloon led Mr Short into the Grand Hall.

The dwarf dropped onto his hands and knees and crawled over to the hole in the skirting board. He

tapped at the wood. They heard goblin laughter.

"Down to business," said Mr Short.

Later that morning, Lord Dubloon returned to the Grand Hall to see how things were going. Mr Short had certainly been busy . All the furniture had been pushed back and covered with dust sheets, and scaffolding had been erected along the wall over the hole in the skirting board.

Pulleys and ropes held a huge net across the roof, and other ropes ran down to the floor, where they were trapped under a large cast iron tub. The tub itself was perched on the end of a plank of wood that was balanced on a barrel like a see-saw.

High above, Lord Dubloon's chair dangled from the scaffolding on a rope. In another corner of the room was a rack of fireworks. Mr Short sat under the scaffolding, slowly fitting together a long, flexible pole.

Lord Dubloon edged across to the tub perched on the see-saw and looked in. It was full of custard.

"Careful there, your Lordship. Custard. Very precarious. This whole apparatus is on a hair trigger."

"What is all this?" asked Lord Dubloon.

"Short's Patent Goblin Trap," replied Mr Short, proudly. "Allow me to explain. They love custard, do goblins, can't get enough of it. They come out of their hole to get to the custard. I light the fireworks. Boom! Bang! Whizz! Very pretty. Goblins love fireworks too. So they're all stood round the custard tub, and they're looking up admiring the fireworks. But ... one of the fireworks is aimed at the rope holding the throne. It cuts through it. The throne drops onto the see-saw, the tub flies into the air, covering the goblins in sticky custard. They can't move, and the net floats down and traps them. Bingo!"

Lord Dubloon nodded, uncertainly. "So why do they come out of the hole in the first place?" he asked. Mr Short held up the long, flexible pole. On the end was a sign that said:

"HEY! GOBLINS! CUSTARD! THIS WAY!"

"This will fetch them out," said Mr Short. "Now, would you be so kind as to poke this pole down the hole?"

Lord Dubloon did so, as Mr Short stood by the fireworks with a lighted match. Lord Dubloon suddenly felt the pole being tugged out of his hands. It disappeared into the hole Hearing excited goblin voices, he backed away. A moment later, a dozen little, green, pointy-eared, fanged, wicked, giggling goblins came rushing out of the skirting board, and headed straight for the custard.

"Bingo!" cried Short, and lit the fireworks. They went off with a bang. It all happened very quickly. The goblins went "Oooohhh!" as they looked up at the fireworks shooting madly around the hall. Then they picked up the tub and ran for the hole in the skirting board.

One firework released the chair, which crashed down and shattered, pinging the see-saw through a window with a loud crash.

The net was already falling. Mr Short, who was being chased by a firework, caught his foot in a stray rope and disappeared up to the ceiling, where he dangled upside down.

Lord Dubloon looked at the devastation that had been his Grand Hall.

He wanted to sit down, but his chair had been smashed into firewood.

Just then, the flexible pole poked back out of the goblin hole with a very badly written note on the end of it.

It read: "tHAnkS FoRe ThE cusTaRd. yor Klown wAs vERy FUnny. mAkE him do It AgAiN."

Fuming, Lord Dubloon looked up at Mr Short. "Bingo?"

"Just a temporary setback, your Lordship," began Mr Short. "Er. . . do you think you could help me down from here?"

Lord Dubloon winced as the echoes of goblin laughter floated out from the skirting board. "I'll make 'short' work of you when I do!"

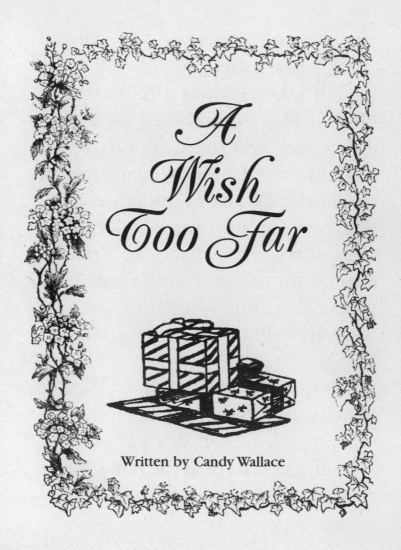

A Wish Too Far

Written by Candy Wallace

NATHAN WAS BORED. He wasn't just bored in that "Ho Hum! I haven't got a thing to do!" kind of way that most of us feel every now and then. Oh no, he was bored in a full blown, major league, top of the list, wet Sunday afternoon in a boring seaside town kind of way, that makes you pace around for an hour and a half before screaming, "IIIIII'm boooorrred!!" at the top of your voice.

Strangely enough, it was a wet Sunday afternoon in a boring seaside town. Nathan's parents had brought him here with talk of a "lovely week in a delightful town by the sea". So far, the "lovely" and "delightful" parts of his parents' description had most definitely failed to appear.

Certainly, they had spent the better part of a week in a town by the sea (which was a distinctly murky shade of grey, by the way), but "lovely" and "delightful"? No, these weren't the words that sprang into Nathan's mind. It had, after all, rained for half the time and poured with rain for the other half.

The gloomy atmosphere that hung over the town was like the feeling you get when you're waiting for a kiss from a particularly ugly, long lost aunt!

Making matters worse was the fact that his little sister, Janine, and his little brother, Christian, were having a lovely time playing happily together. The miserable weather didn't seem to bother them. They were just as happy to play indoors.

Nathan just wanted the holiday to be over and to get back home. Unfortunately, they still had another two days to go.

Nathan paced up and down, sat grumpily in a chair (ignoring the book that his dad had bought for him), or sat in front of the television, flicking between the channels. And still the rain pitter-pattered against the window.

"I wish I could be on my own somewhere, without my family getting under my feet!" he thought, gloomily.

Finally, he got up and grabbed his coat. "Where are you going?" asked his mum.

"Into the garden!" he replied.

His mum sighed wearily. "But it's still raining!"

Nathan put on his coat.

"I don't care!" he said. "I'm going to stand in the garden and grow roots and become a tree and then I'll be stuck here for ever!" And with that, he stomped out.

"Cor!" said Janine, excitedly. "That sounds brilliant! Come on, Chris, let's go and watch!"

Out in the garden, Nathan splashed across the muddy grass with his sister and brother following closely behind. As they neared the far end of the garden, Nathan turned to the others and began to snarl at them, continuing to walk backwards as he did so.

"Why don't you leave me alone?" he snapped.

"We want to see you turn into a tree!" Christian replied.

"Ohhh… that's all I need…" Nathan began, but was cut off as he disappeared from sight. Janine and Christian stopped in their tracks.

They looked down and saw a hole in the ground where Nathan

had been walking. Peering down into it, they jumped back with shock as Nathan's head popped up.

"Aaaaahhhh!" they screamed in unison.

"It's okay!" replied Nathan. "The hole wasn't very deep! And look what I found down there..."

Nathan held up a small, shiny box that gleamed and sparkled, even in the gloomy rain.

"What is it?" Janine asked.

Just as she spoke, the box slipped from Nathan's fingers and landed on the wet grass. The lid flipped open and a twinkly swirl of light flew into the air. The children gasped in amazement, as a tiny figure materialised in front of them. A man, no more than five or six inches tall, hovered in the air before landing on a nearby sunflower. He had a bushy white beard and was wearing a pointed red hat.

"Ohhhh…" he groaned. "My

aching back! I've been in that box for bloomin' years!"

Nathan, eyes and mouth wide with surprise, asked the little man who and what he was.

"I'm Eric!" he stated, puffing out his chest proudly. "Eric the Elf, young sir! You have freed me from a trap set for me a long time ago by a particularly grumpy wizard!"

"You're an elf?!" Nathan said. "That's incredible!"

The little elf looked flattered.

"You said it, young man!" he replied. "I am incredible. And seeing as how you've freed me from that box, and furthermore, seeing as how you seem to be a young man of exceedingly good taste, I will grant you three wishes!"

Barely pausing for thought, Nathan said, "I wish my family would disappear!" With a tinkling of bells, Janine, Christian and their parents promptly vanished. Nathan sat on the wet grass, not quite believing what had happened.

"Is… is that it?" he asked. "Are they r…really gone?"

Eric gestured around the garden. "Look around you !" he said. Certainly, Janine and Christian were no longer there. Eric leant forwards and prodded Nathan. "Listen, sonny, I'm a busy elf! What's your second wish?"

"I wish I was somewhere nice and hot, all by myself!" Nathan answered. And suddenly, he was alone on a beautiful beach, the blue sky arching high over his head and the sea glittering like polished diamonds and stretching away for ever.

"Wow!" Nathan said, getting to his feet and running across the hot sand. "This is brilliant, eh, Eric? Eric?" There was no answer. Nathan whirled around quickly, looking everywhere. "Eric?" he shouted again, but there was no reply, only the sound of the sea, lapping gently at the shore.

He ran around for what seemed

like ages, but the empty beach seemed to have no end, and the tropical forest that bordered the beach looked a bit dark and scary.

Finally, hot, tired and more than a little worried, he flopped down on the sand and began to sob quietly. If only he could be back with all his family around him in that funny little bungalow on the edge of the wet and dreary seaside town!

"Well, I'm sure that can be arranged!" said a little voice at Nathan's side, making him jump. It was Eric. "You said you wanted to be alone, so I thought I'd give you a little time to yourself!"

"I want to go back and I want my family to be back with me!" Nathan said, breathlessly.

"And is that your third and final wish, then?" Eric asked. Nathan nodded his head vigorously.

"Oh, it is! It is!" he said.

"I'll see what I can do," said Eric.

Janine tugged at his arm and

Nathan felt the rain against his face. "Come up out of that hole!" she said, as she and Christian peered down at him. Nathan climbed out of the damp hole and looked around, feeling very glad to be back. He could see his mum and dad inside the house and thought to himself that it was one of the nicest sights he had ever seen.

"Your brother and sister won't remember me!" Eric said, appearing in front of Nathan. "But I think you will, and you'll remember what you learnt today!"

"You bet!" Nathan said. "I'll never take my family for granted again! Even if they do bring me for a lovely week in a delightful town by the sea!"

And as Eric twinkled from sight, Nathan looked up at the grey sky, took his sister's hand, and ran inside laughing to join his family!

Puffcheek's Palace

Written by Geoff Cowan

IF YOU WALK carefully and quietly through a woodland dell, don't be startled to hear faint voices and glimpse some colourfully dressed little people. For there may be elves and pixies about, just like there were in the woods behind the garden of Kate's cottage home. Only, her brother Sam didn't believe her. Then something very strange happened that made him begin to wonder...

"Pull!" cried Topknot, sitting grandly on a small carriage he had found while going early-morning exploring.

He had fetched the other elves, and they were using a rope of woven grass to tow his discovery away. However, nothing much happened in those woods without the sharp-eyed pixies noticing. When they saw the carriage, they wanted to join in the fun.

"Push!" shouted Puffcheek to his fellow pixies.

So the elves pulled the carriage while the pixies pushed, until it lurched and Topknot almost fell off.

"Pulling's safer than pushing me along!" he called, grumpily.

"But pushing's easier, especially if you go downhill!" protested Puffcheek. "Watch! We'll show you!"

Before Topknot could stop them, Puffcheek and the other

pixies gave such a mighty shove that the carriage suddenly sped forward. It moved so fast that the startled elves hardly had time to jump out of the way.

Now, Topknot did topple off. He landed safely and softly on the thick grass while the carriage hurtled into a deep ditch and overturned, its wheels spinning in the air.

"That was your fault, Puffcheek!" snapped Topknot. "When it comes to being useful, pixies should learn a lesson from elves!"

Suddenly, heavy footsteps saved an argument as they all raced for cover.

"There it is!" cried Kate, pointing. "What a place to leave your skateboard!"

"I didn't!" replied Sam. "I told you! I put it down by a tree at the edge of the woods while I collected some conkers that had fallen. I couldn't carry everything home in one go. Then Mum called us for tea and I forgot all about my skateboard until today. Someone must have moved it!"

"Pixies and elves, I suppose!" smiled Kate.

Sam laughed and scrambled into the ditch. He picked up his skateboard, then headed for home. Kate was about to follow when she spotted the elves' grass rope that had broken free from the skateboard. Kate looked at it thoughtfully and put it in her pocket.

"So that's where the carriage came from," said Topknot, afterwards.

"You mean skateboard," corrected Puffcheek. "The Big People use all kinds of odd things and give them some very funny names!"

"Well, whatever they call it, I want it back!" cried Topknot. "Finders keepers. That's only fair!"

Even the pixies agreed, so Puffcheek had no choice but to try and recover the skateboard.

Which brought him to Kate's

cottage garden. Sam had already gone to meet a friend, taking the skateboard with him. Meanwhile, Kate sat at the far end of the garden to examine the little grass rope. Puffcheek crept closer, searching for the skateboard. Suddenly, Kate sneezed and blew the pixie off a log he had clambered on to.

"Hey! Look out, clumsy!" he yelled and Kate was just close enough to hear.

"Oh, there really are pixies," she cried. "Did you make this rope?"

"No, it was the elves!" replied Puffcheek, picking himself up.

Then he remembered how

much larger Big People were and was about to hurry away. It was only the thought of facing an angry Topknot without the skateboard that stopped him.

"I'll weave you a grass bracelet if you give me that carriage, er, skateboard," said Puffcheek.

"I was right! You did move it!" said Kate. "But the skateboard's not mine!"

Puffcheek explained what had happened. Then he sighed, "I can't return empty-handed to Topknot!"

Kate remembered something and had an idea. "Come back as the sun goes down and I may be able to help. "

Unbeknown to Kate, Sam had arrived home and come into the garden.

"Who were you talking to?" he asked Kate, puzzled.

"Oh, just a pixie!" she replied, playfully. "You know you tidied up your cupboard yesterday. Didn't you say you wanted to get rid of your toy castle?" Kate asked.

Sam nodded. "I'm too big for it now!"

"I know someone who's just the right size!" said Kate. "Can I have it?"

"If you like," said Sam.

When Sam went inside, Kate fetched the little castle, complete with its turrets, drawbridge and battlements. She took it to the edge of the wood. At dusk, Puffcheek found the castle with a note from Kate telling him it was for Topknot.

"I'm sorry I was cross with you, Puffcheek!" said Topknot as, this time, the elves and pixies happily pushed and pulled the toy castle deeper into the woods. "A castle's better than a carriage any day!"

"You can call it 'Topknot's Castle'," said Puffcheek.

"Or 'Puffcheek's Palace'," replied Topknot kindly. "It's yours as long as we can play inside and have parties there! After all, you were very brave to speak to one of the Big People!"

Puffcheek smiled proudly as the elves and pixies congratulated him.

Next morning, before school, Sam followed his sister into the garden.

"I saw you carrying my castle

down to the bottom of the garden last night," he said. "You wanted to play with it yourself all along, didn't you?"

"No, I left it here," replied Kate, pointing. "But it's gone!"

"Just like my skateboard," said Sam, thoughtfully. "Shall we search for it?"

"No," replied Kate, who was very pleased to have helped Puffcheek and the others.

"Don't tell me you think the elves and pixies took my old toy castle too!" grinned Sam.

Kate nodded. "Who else?" she smiled. "Only, this time, I think we'll let them keep it!"

Playful
the Pixie

Written by Geoff Cowan

PLAYFUL lived up to his name. That's what the other pixies in the wood called him because he was always playing tricks on them. At first they laughed because pixies do get up to mischief once in a while. But Playful's pranks began to get out of hand.

"Wheee!" he yelled as he suddenly swung on a strand of ivy right towards Picklepot, who was sipping a cup of cold dewdrop tea. It spilt all over him.

"Ooh! Ow!" yelled Sunnysmile, as Playful lay in wait and pelted him with berries. The juice stained Sunnysmile's clothes.

"Grrrgh!" spluttered an unsuspecting Curlytoes when he pulled on his hat and found Playful had filled it with water. Truth was, the pixies were more than a little tired of Playful's non-stop naughtiness. Time and again they asked him to behave.

"A joke's a joke but you've gone too far, Playful," they warned.

"Or not far enough!" grumbled some. "Keep this up and you can go and play in someone else's patch of wood!"

Which is exactly what Playful did. One morning, he climbed out of bed extra early and set off across the meadow into another

wood where a band of elves lived.
And what a dance he led them, too.
Playful made sure he kept himself
hidden and puffed pollen on the
elves to make them sneeze. While
they slept, he swapped their boots
around so they didn't fit!

"This is better fun than before," giggled Playful. "Now no one even knows it's me!"

That was until the elves caught him, for elves are much more clever than you might think. They knew someone had to be behind all the odd goings-on, so they laid a trap.

Playful fell for it; or it fell for Playful, to be exact. A carefully placed bag of honey dropped on his hat, bursting open, the next time he tried to creep up on the elves.

"Caught you!" they cried, feeling extremely pleased with themselves as they danced around a very gooey Playful.

"Mess with us and you'll come unstuck!" warned an elf named Echo. He was called Echo because he liked the sound of his own voice.

"I'm in a mess and all stuck up!" cried Playful, miserably.

"Serves you right!" sang Echo. "When you're washed and clean, we'll take you back where you came from."

One of the elves had guessed
Playful was from The Other Wood
because he'd heard it was full of
pixies. When both bands came face
to face, the pixies were startled to
see Playful with the elves. They
weren't so surprised to hear about
all the bother he'd caused.

"The least we can do is invite
you to a Pixie Party," Picklepot told
the elves. "There'll be music,
dancing and all the pixie pizzas
you can eat!"

And more of Playful's pranks.
The fact was he just couldn't seem
to help himself. He sprinkled mud
on the mushroom seats to make
folk sit down with a squelch! He

put jelly in a flower-trumpet so
wobbly bits were blown out everywhere when the pixie band played;
and that was only the start.

The elves and pixies were fed
up before they'd even eaten
anything! When they did sit down
to eat they were furious to
discover that someone had mixed
up all the food and put mustard in
the jam sandwiches and tomato
ketchup in the sponge cake. Things
had gone beyond a joke!

It called for quick thinking
before tempers flared. Picklepot
and Echo drew up a plan. The first
part was easy. For the rest of the
party, the elves and pixies would

take it in turns to watch Playful
very carefully. If he showed the
slightest sign of mischief, they
would step in and stop him. The
second part was harder...

Next morning, when Playful
woke, what do you think his first
thought of the day was? Which
new tricks he should try out, of
course! But he never got the
chance to play any tricks, because
he realised with a terrible shock
that he had no idea where he was.

And even worse, he was all alone. He was in a part of the wood he had never been to before.

"Trembling toadstools! Where am I?" gasped Playful, sitting up with a start. "Where is everyone?"

Before Playful could throw back his patchwork blanket, it flew off as if by magic, leaving him lying in his night-shirt.

"What's happening?" gasped Playful, reaching for the folded green tunic on the end of the bed. He went to pull it on and found he couldn't. It was much too tiny!

"Hey! That's not mine!" he cried, crossly.

At least the boots fitted but

these weren't his either and they had big holes in the soles. Next moment, Playful spotted a folded piece of paper on the ground. His name was written on it in large

letters. As Playful hurried to pick it up, the paper danced into the air then settled close by.

Playful hoped there might be a map on the other side to show him the way home. But every time he neared the paper, it fluttered further away until it landed long

enough to Playful to pounce.
Whoosh! A net hidden under some
leaves sprang up and closed around
him. Playful was whisked off his
feet and found himself dangling in
mid-air.

"Caught you!" cried a voice as
Playful struggled.

"Let me down, whoever you
are! Please stop playing tricks on
me!" he called, dizzily. He was really
rather frightened indeed.

"Only if you stop playing them
on all of us!" said Picklepot, who
stepped out from behind a tree
with the other pixies.

"And us! And us!" repeated
Echo who appeared with the elves.

"Yes! I promise!" said Playful, who was relieved to see them. They gently lowered the net and helped him out.

Now Playful noticed Sunnysmile holding the bed blanket tied to a long thread that he had used to pull it away. Another was tied to the note Playful had chased to lure him to the net. Curlytoes happily handed over Playful's proper clothes.

"We carried your bed here while you slept," grinned Picklepot. "Then we set up the other tricks."

"They're not funny when someone plays them on you, are they?" said Echo sternly.

"I hadn't thought of that," agreed Playful, shaking his head. "It isn't very nice, is it? I promise that from today I won't play any more tricks on anyone. Except maybe just a small one on Sundays."

The elves and the pixies all chuckled, and Picklepot said that was good enough for him. The elves agreed and returned to their own wood. From that day on, Playful was the best-behaved pixie you could imagine — except on Sundays, when everyone wondered who's turn it would be for him to play tricks on!

The pixies even gave him a new name 'Goodasgold', and he

became a very helpful little pixie indeed.

So if you ever chance to meet a very polite pixie, remember who it could be and be careful never to ask him, "How's tricks?!"

Especially on a Sunday!

Trading Places

Written by Amber Hunt

KATINA HATED being a pixie. Her parents said it was a pixie's job to look after the woodland they lived in, but Katina thought that was boring. What she really wanted to be was a Tooth Fairy and to dress in beautiful fairy clothes and carry a wand, some fairy dust, and the special Tooth Fairy bag. But Katina was a pixie, so she wiped the dew off the grass and polished the leaves and painted and scented the flowers and all the time she was fed up, bored and grumpy.

In fact, Katina was so grumpy that all her friends had started flying away when they saw her. So now Katina was not only fed up, bored and grumpy, but also lonely too.

Then, early one sunny morning, when Katina was naughtily painting a flower a particularly nasty shade of yucky purple and scenting it with a really horrible smell, she thought she heard someone crying.

Katina stopped and listened. There it was again, someone was definitely crying.

"Well, tough," she thought. "Nobody cares that I'm miserable, so why should I care just because someone is crying," and she went back to what she was doing.

But the crying didn't stop and eventually Katina's curiosity got the better of her and she went to have a look.

It was coming from a clump of bluebells. Well, they would have been blue if Katina hadn't painted them a sickly green yellow. They should have smelled nice too, but they didn't.

Katina tip-toed up to the smelly clump of greeny-yellow bells and peeped through.

There behind them was … a Tooth Fairy!

"Gosh," said Katina. "A Tooth Fairy! Why are you crying?"

"Because I'm upset, stupid," snapped the Tooth Fairy.

"Oh well, fine," said Katina, "if that's how you feel, you can jolly well go on crying," and she went to fly off.

"No wait," said the fairy. "I'm sorry, I'm not usually rude. It's just that I've sprained my wing and I can't fly." Turning round she showed Katina her hurt wing.

"Oh," said Katina. "What are you going to do?"

"I don't know," sniffed the fairy. "I'm supposed to be visiting a little girl and we never let children down. But there's only a short time left before the little girl wakes up. She'll be so disappointed if her tooth is still there and there's no coin." The fairy started crying again.

"Oh, for goodness sake," said Katina. "Do stop. I'll take you to see my mum and dad. I expect they'll know what to do."

Katina helped the fairy out of the greeny-yellow bells. "What's that horrid smell?" asked the fairy. "And

why are those flowers such a
revolting colour?"

"Oh, a naughty pixie did that,"
explained Katina.

"Dreadful," said the fairy. "I
hope you don't do things like that."
She gave Katina a long hard stare .

As they walked along, Katina
suddenly stopped in her tracks.
"I've got an idea," she gasped,
amazed at her own daring. "I can

fly, so why don't I take the coin to the little girl for you and bring you back her tooth? Please let me," she begged.

The fairy looked at Katina thoughtfully, "All right," she said eventually. "There isn't much time though, and you must do exactly as I say." She gave Katina precise instructions and made Katina repeat them back to her three times before she was satisfied. Finally, she gave Katina the special Tooth Fairy bag and sent her on her way.

Katina flew through the woodland bursting with joy. If she did this well, perhaps she would be allowed to become a Tooth Fairy one day.

The Tooth Fairy sat and waited, feeling rather worried. Then, as the sun was rising further in the sky and it was approaching the time when humans wake up, Katina returned. She flew to the fairy's side and collapsed in a panting, dirty and rather smelly heap.

"I did it," she gasped, holding out the bag to the fairy, and then added, "Is it always like that?"

"Like what, exactly?" asked the fairy.

"Well," said Katina, "I flew out of the woodland and in the direction you said, when suddenly

there was a terrible noise and this
huge horrible monster came
screaming right at me. I flew for my
life and barely escaped."

The fairy nodded knowingly
and said, "I think you will find that
was one of the cars I warned you
about. They are very dangerous, but
they never leave the road the
humans built for them to run on."

"Oh," said Katina, impressed by the fairy's knowledge. "Then I was chased by a big hairy monster with enormous eyes, massive fangs and hot evil smelling breath."

The fairy laughed.

"That was a dog. They are friendly and mostly they just want to play, but you have to be careful that you don't accidentally get squashed by them."

"After that," went on Katina, "I was chased by another, smaller monster. This one had big green eyes, sharp teeth and claws and it hissed at me. I had to hide in a smelly hill near the little girl's house, until it went away."

"Ah," sighed the fairy, "that was a cat. You have to be careful with cats. Sometimes they just want to play, but sometimes they can be very spiteful. You were wise to hide, although I suspect that what you hid in was called a compost heap. You really do smell quite unpleasant you know."

"Thanks a lot," sniffed Katina.

"You know," the Tooth Fairy went on, "since you've done so well the Grand Fairy Committee might consider allowing you to attend the Tooth Fairy School."

Katina smiled. "No thank you," she said. "I thought I wanted to be a Tooth Fairy, but after today, I've

decided I'm very happy being a
pixie.

"And no more nasty coloured
flowers with horrible smells?"
asked the fairy.

"Ah," said Katina, "you knew.
No," she promised, "and I won't be
grumpy any more either."

The fairy nodded, pleased, and
gave Katina a big hug. Then, arm in
arm, they went off through the
woodland. The Tooth Fairy's wing

soon recovered and she became the best of friends with Katina, who kept her little patch of woodland spotless.

Wobbly Witch

Written by Candy Wallace

WOBBLY WITCH had a problem. She was wobbly. She wasn't wobbly when she walked down to the bottom of the garden to pick toadstools. And she wasn't wobbly when she stood over her cauldron mixing the latest recipes from *What Spell?* magazine, or when she sat on her little stool by the fire and toasted rats' tails for tea. But, when she tried to fly anywhere on her broomstick — she wobbled. She wobbled and swayed and clutched and shrieked and fell to the ground in a horrible heap!

Poor Wobbly had never learned to fly a broomstick. Some witches took to it like a duck to water and never needed a single lesson. Others went to the *Sky's The Limit School of Broomstick Flying*. But Wobbly just couldn't be bothered to learn when she was young and now she was too proud to admit that she couldn't fly. She told all her friends that she'd lost her broomstick.

So Wobbly had to go everywhere on the bus. It was very embarrassing and most inconvenient. How would you feel if you had to sit on a bus in your pointy black hat with horrid schoolboys making rude remarks about your funny nose? She even had to go to the W.I. (the Witches' Institute) on the bus. All the others flew in on smart broomsticks. Wobbly felt quite left out as they discussed the special features of their latest models.

"Mine does 0–60 in ten seconds," said Edna.

Wobbly might never have learned to fly, if it hadn't been for the birthday present and her cat, Boris.

On Wobbly's birthday the postman brought lots of lovely birthday cards, a couple of small parcels and one big one that was very long and very thin. One parcel had a smart new witch's hat in it, from Wobbly's friend Vera.

The other one was a silver balloon on a string. It had "Happy Birthday!" on it and floated up into the air when she opened the parcel. Wobbly was very pleased.

"Now what can this long one be, Boris?" said Wobbly to her cat, who, like all cats was very curious. Boris snuggled up to Wobbly and purred. He'd had a large kipper for breakfast and was in a very good mood.

Wobbly opened the long thin parcel and her heart sank to her big black boots. It was a spanking new, super deluxe broomstick with built-in stereo and cat seat! "To Wobbly," said the card, "with love from all your friends at the Witches' Institute."

Wobbly hurriedly wrapped it up again and stuffed the broomstick under the bed. "Stupid present," she muttered. "I hate birthdays." And she didn't cheer up until Boris rolled on his back and made her chuckle.

That night the W.I. were meeting. Wobbly went on the bus, as usual.

"I'll tell them I forgot my broomstick," she said to herself. When she arrived, there was a big surprise — her friends had laid on a lovely birthday party for her.

"Happy Birthday, Wobbly!" they shouted as she came in the door.

"Where's your lovely new broomstick?"

Wobbly soon forgot to feel
miserable. There was a huge
birthday cake decorated with little
bats made out of icing. There were
extra wobbly jellies in her honour
and lots of delicious sandwiches. It
all went well, until somebody
mentioned playing games.

They played Hide and Shriek,
Pass the Toad and Pin the Tail on
the Rat. But the next game was
Broomstick Races. Soon, all the
witches but Wobbly were whizzing
up and down on their broomsticks,
cackling and having fun. Wobbly
looked on and sulked.

"Right, that's it!" she said. "I'm going home. I hate parties!" And she sneaked out. When she arrived home, she expected Boris to meet her at the door. But there was no sign of him.

"Great lazy lump," thought Wobbly, crossly. "He's still sleeping off that kipper I gave him!" But when she looked on his favourite chair, he wasn't there. "Boris, Boris,

where are you?" she called. But there was no answering miaow.

Feeling worried, Wobbly went outside and called his name again. It was a dark night with a bright, shiny moon and she strained her eyes to see. Then something caught her eye. Right at the top of a tree, she saw a flash of light. It was her birthday balloon, caught on a branch. Suddenly, the branch shook.

"Miaeeeeew!" It was Boris! He had chased the balloon to the top of the tallest tree in the garden and now he was stuck!

"Oh, you silly cat!" shrieked Wobbly. "How am I going to get you down from there!"

"Miaeeeeeew!" wailed poor Boris.

Wobbly rushed to fetch an old ladder. But when she put it against the tree it didn't even reach half way up. Poor Boris seemed to be clinging on by a claw. His miaows grew fainter…

Wobbly stamped her foot and turned and rushed into her cottage. She dashed up the stairs and into the bedroom.

On her hands and knees, she grabbed the parcel under the bed and hurried downstairs with it, tearing off the paper as she went.

"Don't worry, Boris!" she cried. "I'll rescue you!" Leaping astride the gleaming new broomstick, she closed her eyes and took a deep breath…

Up she went, up into the sky without a single wobble! As she climbed higher and higher, her old hat blew off and was carried away by the wind. The broomstick swept round in a curve and came to a stop, hovering over the branch where poor Boris was clinging on for dear life.

Wobbly grabbed him and put him on the broomstick behind her. Then she untangled the balloon, tied it to the broomstick and swept down to a smooth landing outside her front door. Boris walked off the broomstick as if nothing had happened.

Wobbly leapt off and skipped and hopped with glee.

"Did you see that, Boris!" she cackled. "I can fly, I can fly! Come on!" She ran into the cottage and grabbed her new hat. "We have a party to go to!"

They jumped back on and took off.

"I've fetched my new broom-stick!" cried Wobbly as she arrived at the party. They were still racing broomsticks and hadn't even noticed she was gone! Wobbly and Boris joined in and won two races! As they flew home after the party,

Wobbly looked down at the bus below and chuckled.

"I couldn't fly because I was afraid," she said to Boris, who sat purring behind her. "But tonight I

was so worried you would fall and
hurt yourself — I forgot to be
afraid!"

From that day on, Wobbly flew
everywhere on her smart new
broomstick. She's still called
Wobbly, but she doesn't wobble any
more!

Magic Mix-up

Written by Claire Steeden

ONE SUNNY MORNING Wanda the Witch woke up, rubbed her eyes and climbed out of her rather saggy bed. She put on her favourite black dress with purple stars. It was quite tatty as she wore it every day. She tied a belt round her plump belly and pulled on her shoes with curly wurly toes. Then she pushed her hair up into her pointy hat as it was so tangled she could not get a brush through it. She looked in the mirror and laughed.

"What a mess. Still, I've no time to waste on myself."

Wanda was always busy doing spells for her friends. Her 'rock into enormous sticky chocolate pudding' spell was frequently in demand. However, her wand had never been quite the same since it had fallen into her cauldron and her spells often got in a muddle.

This morning Wanda had an important spell to do. Harriet the Hedgehog was having a birthday party for her son Harry that afternoon, and Wanda was making a special cake. She lifted her enormous book of spells off the shelf, popped her glasses on her long nose and peered at the first page.

"Bestest birthday cakes," she read out, "page seventy-three."

She turned the pages filled
with magic. "Let's see what we
need. One large frog, got that, a cup
of rats' tails, got that, some slimy
slugs, got them, and a pretty,
scented flower for decoration.
Bother, I haven't got one of those.
Mix together, throw mixture into
the air, wave your wand and say the
magic words:

 'Up in the air, twist and shake,
 Make me the bestest birthday
cake.'

Well that sounds simple. I just need to go and pick a flower." Wanda put on her shawl and bustled down the garden path and into the forest, where she found a small bush with the prettiest flowers. Wanda bent down to pick one, held it under her nose to sniff and tucked it into her pocket.

As she stood up she heard someone humming close by. Wanda crept behind a huge oak tree. Peeping out, she saw the beautiful Princess Primula, who had long golden curly hair, big brown eyes, dainty little hands and a gorgeous sparkly pink gown. Wanda looked down at herself and realised how

shabby and ugly she was. At that
moment Princess Primula rounded
the tree and came face to face with
Wanda. The princess let out an
almighty scream and ran away as
fast as she could.

"I must have really scared her.
She is so beautiful and I'm so ugly."
A tear rolled down Wanda's cheek.
Then she had an idea. "I'm always
doing magic for other people. I
should do some for myself. I'll go
home and make myself as beautiful
as the princess."

Picking up her skirt she ran as
fast as her short fat legs could carry
her. Wanda flicked through her
book of spells and found a spell to

make lovely long hair. She took off
her hat, picked up her wand and
said the magic words:

"*Take away this tangled mess,*
and in its place put hair.
As long and fine as it can be,
to make me look most fair."

But when she felt her head,
instead of soft silky hair, she felt
something smooth and shiny. She
was completely bald!

"Oh bother," she cried. "This stupid wand. I'll have to buy a new one the next time I go to Witch-ways. Oh well, I'll come back to my hair later. I think I'll try making my hands and feet smaller."

Wanda found the right spell and read it out carefully.
"My hands and feet are far too big,
I'd like them to be tiny.
With skin as soft as purest silk,
And nails all long and shiny."

But, oh dear, when Wanda held out her arms there at the end were two dainty little feet.

When she stuck out her legs there were two pretty hands on the end of each. "Drat and blast. What a muddle. Oh well, I'll sort them out later."

Wanda decided to try to make her nose and chin less pointed.

She read out the spell:
"Go away you pointy nose,
*   and you pointy chin.*
Instead be nice and rounded,
*   pretty, small and trim."*

She waved her wand above her head and hoped the spell had worked. But, oh dear, guess what happened. A very pretty little nose appeared, but not where a nose should be. It was on her chin, which was now much smaller.

"I'm really getting in a muddle. I'll try one more time, then I'd better sort out all those mixed-up spells. I think I'll try a spell to make me thinner."

"Bulges on my belly,
bulges on my thighs.
Go away and don't come back,
please be a smaller size."

With a wave of her wand she was instantly so thin that her dress

fell off her shoulders and onto the floor. Wanda was left standing in the kitchen in just her underwear!

At that moment Harriet the Hedgehog knocked at the door and came in. She took one look at Wanda and burst into a fit of giggles. "What on earth are you doing?"

"I was trying to make myself beautiful," replied Wanda.

"Well, it looks like things have gone a bit wrong. Go and look at yourself in the mirror," giggled Harriet.

Wanda stood in front of her mirror and started to laugh.

"Oh dear, this really isn't quite

what I had in mind. What a muddle," said Wanda.

"Why do you want to look beautiful?" asked Harriet. Wanda explained what had happened in the forest.

"Well, I don't know why you're making such a fuss. Although Princess Primula is beautiful on the outside, she's horrible inside. She's mean and selfish and nobody likes her," explained Harriet. "You may not be beautiful but you are kind and helpful and everybody loves you."

Wanda thought about this. "Yes, I do have lots of friends and that is more important than being beautiful. I'd better get out of this muddle and get on with Harry's cake."

Wanda cancelled all the spells, put her dress back on and turned to the birthday cake spell. She mixed the ingredients in her cauldron, threw the mixture in the air, and said the magic words:

"Up in the air, twist and shake.
Make me the bestest
birthday cake."

She waved her wand and there on the table appeared the biggest, gooiest, most scrummy cake you have ever seen.

"At last a spell that's worked! Now I'd better hurry and get ready,

the party will be starting soon."
Wanda decided to make a real
effort to look the best she could,
but without using any magic this
time! She had a bath, washed her
hair and even managed to brush it.
She put on a new sparkly blue
dress with gold moons, and a pair
of purple satin boots. She looked in
the mirror and smiled.

"I'm not so ugly after all," she
said to herself. "But I realise now
that being beautiful inside is more
important."

When she arrived at the party
everyone marvelled at the cake and
her friends told her how lovely she
looked. After Harry had opened all

of his presents he handed Wanda a
parcel.

"But it's not my birthday," she
said.

"I know. But we all wanted to
buy you something to show you
how much we love you," said Harry.

Wanda unwrapped the present
and there inside was a wonderful
new wand. "You won't get your

spells muddled now," laughed Harriet. Wanda thanked them all and felt very lucky to have so many friends. She spent the afternoon doing spells with her new wand, entertaining everyone at the party, and of course, eating lots of cake!

A Dog Named Brian

Written by Candy Wallace

WIMPLE THE WITCH was having trouble with her cat. Now, as you know, all witches need a cat. No cat, no spells. They just won't work without the magic spark from a cat's eyes. So when Wimple had trouble with her cat — it was big trouble.

"You're a great big useless heap of fur," she shrieked at Montgomery, who was lying on his back with his paws in the air, snoring. "Can't you think of anything better to do than sleep all day?"

Wimple drew back her large foot and booted him across the room — no mean feat since Montgomery weighed nearly as much as a sack of coal. Montgomery rotated in mid-air twice and came to rest on his paws with a faint look of surprise.

His feelings were more hurt than anything. True, he had slowed down a trifle lately, but frankly, he was getting on a bit now. He'd used up eight-and-a-half lives and all he wanted was a bit of peace.

Wimple put her hands on her hips and glowered at Montgomery, who had keeled over on the spot and fallen into an instant slumber.

"Right!" she screamed. "That's it!" It was time to get another cat. One she could rely on. In two shakes of a rat's tail she was astride her broomstick and on her way to the *Paws for Thought* cat agency.

"I want a sleek, hardworking black cat with a flash of genius. Experience in turning princes into frogs and vice versa would be preferred," she said, to the bored-looking witch behind the counter.

"No," the assistant said.

"What do you mean — no?" said Wimple.

"No cats left on our books. We've had a run on them this week."

Wimple turned purple.

"All we've got left is a dog called Brian." While Wimple stood there, speechless, the assistant went into a back room and came back with a huge bloodhound who looked rather depressed. He knew just what would happen. They always took one look at him and shrieked with laughter.

He'd spent three years learning to be a Witch's Personal Assistant and now nobody would hire him.

"I'll take him!" said Wimple suddenly. She was a desperate witch. "I just wish he wasn't quite so big."

The first problem was that there was no way Brian was going to ride on the broomstick. When he got on it it just wouldn't budge. So poor Wimple had to walk all the way home, carrying her broomstick with Brian lolloping along behind.

Back home, she decided to try him out straight away on a spell. She had an excellent recipe brewing in the cauldron, designed to turn bacon sandwiches into roast beef with roast potatoes,

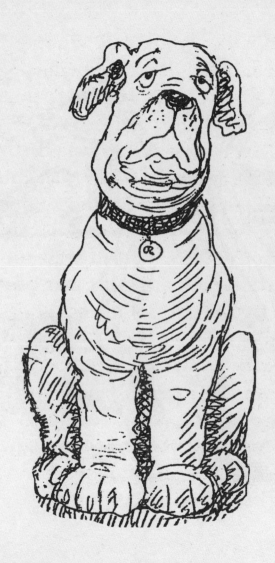

Yorkshire pudding and Brussel sprouts, her favourite meal.

"Right — er — Brian, all you have to do is sit there and stare at the cauldron until it starts to bubble." Brian looked quietly confident. He'd passed Cauldron Staring with grade A.

"I'll go and find that good-for-nothing cat and tell him he's fired!"

Brian sat and stared dutifully at the cauldron. It was a very big cauldron and even Brian couldn't see inside it. So he didn't know whether it was bubbling or not. He thought he'd better check and put his paws up on the top of the cauldron to look in. The big pot swayed and tilted and crash! It toppled over. All the bubbling liquid flowed onto the floor — and over Montgomery who was busy escaping from Wimple.

Montgomery felt very strange for a minute and then turned into a Brussel sprout. Wimple, following behind, stopped dead in her tracks.

"You stupid dog! Quick, we'll have to mix another spell." She thumbed through her recipe book until she found Brussel Sprout — Into Cat, page 62. "We need some toadstools. Go and get some this minute!" Poor Brian was feeling very embarrassed and loped off into the garden, determined he would prove himself this time. He came back carrying a basket full of toadstools.

Strangely enough, Wimple didn't seem pleased. She was staring out of the window with eyes like saucers, clenching her fists.

"You've — just — trampled — all — over — my — magic — herbs," she said, very slowly. "The

ones that have taken me a year to grow…"

Brian thought that now would be a good time to disappear for a while.

When Wimple had calmed down, she mixed the spell, muttering to herself about stupid dogs and cats, and managed to restore Montgom-ery to his previous furry self, none the worse for wear. But then she dropped her recipe book into the cauldron and it disintegrated in a puff of smoke.

That was the last straw. Wimple was literally hopping mad. She jumped up and down and stamped her feet, hopping all over the room.

Then bump! Her head hit the shelf where she kept all her secret jars and bottles.

A big dusty jar marked Frog Mixture teetered on the brink, then fell over, the thick green liquid pouring down onto Wimple's head.

When Brian and Montgomery crept in a little later, Wimple didn't seem to be there. There was just this small, rather bewildered frog sitting on the floor.

Brian looked up at the shelf where all the bottles were higgledy piggledy and saw the upturned jar. He looked at Montgomery and Montgomery looked at him. Then they both looked at the frog.

They ran over to where Wimple's recipe book was kept, but there was no sign of it anywhere! Brian and Montgomery would just have to try and remember the right spell between them. Montgomery rushed out into the garden and nibbled off some squashed herbs. Brian took down the jar marked Pickled Slugs and another that said

All Purpose Slime — Top Quality. They mixed all the ingredients together in a spare pot and stirred it with their paws. The frog looked on and blinked silently. Together, the cat and dog sat and stared hard at the pot. Slowly, it began to bubble. With that, the frog made a sudden leap and landed in the pot with a plop.

And out came — Wimple! She was a little slimy, to be sure, but it was definitely her. When she'd dried herself off and had a couple of chocolate biscuits, she felt much better. Wimple sat on her wooden stool and patted Montgomery and Brian on the head.

"I was wrong about you two," she said finally. "A witch couldn't have two better assistants." She shuddered as she remembered sitting on the floor with green skin and big feet. She would never turn anyone into a frog again. After she'd thrown away all the frog mixture she could find, she found a big juicy bone for Brian and a tasty kipper for Montgomery. "What a team!" she cackled and tucked in to her roast beef and Yorkshire pudding.

The Worst Witches

Written by Ian Tabor

THE WITCHES **Mog, Marge** and **Mable** were useless. If they tried to turn someone into a frog, he turned into a prince and if they tried to turn someone into a prince he turned into a frog. At Witch School they had only been given their diplomas so that they wouldn't come back the following year.

Now they sat round a boiling cauldron in a forest clearing looking extremely down in the mouth.

"I do wish that we could do something right for once," wailed Mog.

"The trouble is," said Marge,

"almost everyone has heard how useless we are. Nobody in their right mind would employ us."

"Hey, listen to this," said Mable letting out a cackle. "DRAGON HOLDS KING TO RANSOM. A mad fire-breathing dragon is rampaging through the land burning all trees before him. The dragon, known simply as Inferno, has said that he will only stop when the king gives him his daughter's hand in marriage. The king has refused and has called on all the brave knights in the kingdom to slay the dragon."

"Ooh!" exclaimed Mog. "We haven't had a dragon in the area for ages. What fun!"

"Not if he's burning down all of our trees it isn't!" said Marge.

"Well if you ask me," said Mable, "this is our chance to show everyone that we're not just three useless old witches. We must stop the dragon, then we'll be heroines."

"But how?"

"Good question. Tell you what, why don't we have a think over a bowl of my nice soup." And giving the cauldron one final stir Mable ladled the thick, green soup into three bowls. "What exactly is in this?" asked Marge, peering cautiously into her bowl, which was boiling and bubbling.

"Oh a little bit of this and a

little bit of that," replied Mable mysteriously. "It's actually a new recipe that I've just made up."

The three witches sipped their soup, trying to think of a way to destroy the evil dragon.

"What's that?" said Mog, looking up from her bowl of soup.

"What's what?" asked Marge.

"That sound. It's a flap, flap, flapping sort of a noise," Mog said, nervously.

"I can hear it as well," said Mable. "But where's it coming from?"

The noise was getting louder and louder. Suddenly Mog let out a piercing scream and pointed to the sky.

Marge and Mable followed her warty finger and there, above them, was the dragon.

"Run!" screamed Mog. "Run before we're fried!" In a mad panic they tried to run away from the monster but all they succeeded in doing was running into each other. Their bowls of soup went flying through the air and landed in the forest. Mog, Marge and Mable ended up in a jumbled heap on the ground.

The dragon swooped down letting out a scorching jet of fire. The witches screamed, but it was too late. Just as the flame was about to reach them and turn them into cinders the three witches fainted.

When Mog woke up she couldn't believe her eyes. The forest was just a smoldering lump of charcoal, all that is, except for three trees.

"Marge! Mable! Wake up!" she cried, poking the other two. "We didn't get burnt. We're alive."

The other two sat up, blinking in disbelief.

"And look," said Mog, pointing to the unharmed trees. "How do you think they survived?"

"It's a miracle!" exclaimed Mable.

"Close," said Marge. "It was your soup, Mable. Look. There's one of our soup bowls at the bottom of each tree. It might not be all that wonderful for eating,"Marge said with a smile, "but your soup makes things fire-proof. You're a genius, Mable!"

"I am?" said Mable, looking at Marge in amazement.

"This is our chance to be heroines," said Marge. "If we can protect the trees, then the dragon's powers will be useless."

"Come on," said Mog. "We haven't a moment to lose. We must go and see the king."

The king was feeling very miserable when the witches arrived and willingly agreed to their plan. All of his knights had ended in a puddle of melted metal. The witches were his last chance.

Huge cauldrons were brought up from the royal kitchens and Mable, with the help of Mog and Marge, began making the special soup. Soon they had made over one hundred cauldrons full of soup. The king gave orders for one drop to be dripped on every tree in the kingdom and for each person to be given one mouthful.

The next time the dragon came he got quite a surprise. He huffed and he puffed but he couldn't get even one small tree to catch alight. In the end he gave up and went back to his lair cursing the witches. The king was overjoyed.

"Well done! Well done indeed!" he exclaimed. "Not only have you saved all the trees in the kingdom, but my daughter will not have to marry that evil dragon. You are now my official royal witches."

Mog, Marge and Mable grinned in delight. Perhaps they weren't so useless after all.

Monster Mayhem

Written by Claire Steeden

IN A GROUP OF CAVES, in the heart
of a dark, dark forest, there once
lived a collection of marvellous
monsters. In one of the caves lived
Rugged Red. He was terribly vain
and spent nearly all day long
looking at himself in the mirror. In
fact, he did not have just one
mirror, but hundreds of them. So
wherever he turned he could see
his reflection.

He loved his deep ruby red
colour and told himself often how
marvellous he looked. He was
particularly proud of the smooth
red spikes that stuck out all over
his body.

Every day he would sit in his

cave, turning his head this way and that, admiring his reflection.

"Oh, you are so handsome," he would say to himself.

He would try all different sorts of hairstyles and pull a number of faces to see which expressions made him look his best.

Now, this in itself was bad enough, but all of Rugged's neighbours were exactly the same, if not worse. They all thought that they were the most handsome or beautiful monster in the world. As you can imagine, they were always arguing about who was the loveliest colour or who had the most attractive hairstyle.

Perfect Purple thought that her purple curls were absolutely fabulous. Brilliant blue, with his shiny scales, said that he was the most breathtaking monster of all. While Awesome Orange argued that his ringlets were the most remarkable of all.

Now, one day, Gorgeous Green, who was the Great Governor of the monsters, got fed up with listening to all the arguing and fighting, so she thought of a cunning plan to put a stop to it, once and for all. She decided to give a huge party and invite all the monsters. She made a long list and sent out posh invitations. Each one matched the colour of the monster she was inviting.

All the monsters were very excited. Wherever you went all you could hear were monsters arguing about who would look the best at the party. Even a few monsters that were not usually as vain as the others fell out with their friends.

The whole place buzzed with excitement. The hairdressers were busy. The Spike Specialists were fully booked. The Scale Scrapers were overrun with customers, not to mention the Claw Clippers and Fang Filers.

The air was filled with talk about colour and style, and size and shape — what a hullabaloo. The monsters argued and preened and shouted and screamed until the noise was unbearable.

When it was nearly time for the party to start the monsters began to queue outside the gates of Gorgeous Green's garden. Together they formed a rainbow of colours — red, yellow, pink, green, orange, purple and blue. It was a splendid sight to see them all standing next to each other.

At two o'clock the gates were opened and the monsters filed in. As they entered they were each given a sparkling drink which tasted very unusual. It kept

changing colour, and tiny coloured bubbles rose from the top.

Gorgeous Green had decorated her garden with balloons and streamers, and lots and lots of mirrors.

Finally, all the monsters arrived and the party got underway. There were long tables full of scrummy things to eat and a big bowl of punch, which looked delicious.

Gorgeous Green had organised party games and had hired a band to play all their favourite monster music.

It had all the ingredients of a perfect party, except for one thing. None of the monsters were interested in the food, the party games or the music. They were all much too busy looking at their reflections and arguing about who was the nicest colour.

Gorgeous Green had known that this would happen. She knew how unfriendly and vain all the monsters were and she was tired of seeing everyone so miserable. The monsters had forgotten how to have fun.

She stood on a platform and signalled to the band to stop playing. Then she spoke to the monsters.

"I have invited you to my party for a special reason. I have been watching and listening to you all for a long time. It makes me sad to see you fighting, especially when there is no reason to. You are all wonderful, and nobody is a nicer colour than anyone else."

With this all the monsters started talking at once. How could she say such a thing? It was ridiculous!

"Please listen. I invited you here to have fun and enjoy yourselves, but you are all too busy arguing. Well, I knew that talking to you wouldn't stop you from quarrelling, so I asked Wizzle the Wizard to make me a magic potion. As you came in you all drank a glass of his potion, and I'm glad to see that it has started to work. Go and look at yourselves in the mirrors."

With that, the monsters turned to look at their reflections, and guess what had happened!

Instead of seeing a blue monster, or a yellow monster in the mirror, they were grey. Every single monster had turned grey! They gasped and turned to Gorgeous Green in astonishment.

"I thought that if everyone looked the same, there would be nothing more to argue about. Now you can enjoy the party and have fun with your friends."

The monsters looked down at

themselves and then at each other. One by one they realised how silly they had been. All that time they had wasted when they could have been having fun.

The band started to play and Gorgeous Green, who was also grey by now, organised lots of games to play.

All the monsters had a wonderful afternoon. None of them could remember when they had had such a good time. They played, and danced and ate and laughed and sang. Gorgeous Green felt very happy. Her plan had worked. The monsters had stopped arguing at last.

Again she stood up to speak to them.

"This afternoon I think you've learnt a very important lesson. Now you can see that being a different colour doesn't matter. We are all friends because we like each other and nobody is better than anyone else. Since you have learnt your lesson, I think it's time to change back to our original colours. If you each have a glass of the punch on this table, you will turn back to the colour you were."

Everyone drank the punch and started to change back slowly. But this time they did not argue. They carried on with the party late into the night. Nobody wanted to go home, they all wanted to stay and have fun with their new found friends!

A Monster Hit

Written by Candy Wallace

IT WAS a Tuesday when Kevin discovered there was a monster living in the television. He had just settled down to watch his favourite cartoon programme with a ginormous glass of lemonade and a jumbo packet of crisps.

Reggie the cat had been sleeping peacefully on the rug, ears and whiskers twitching as he dreamed happily of a wrestling match with a giant mouse, where, as usual, the score was Reggie 1, Mouse 0. Everything normal then, in Kevin's house.

Kevin took a huge mouthful of crisps and a big gulp of lemonade and settled down to watch *The*

Adventures of Fancy Frog, a gripping tale of a gentleman frog who wore a spotted bow tie and carried a walking cane.

This week, he was doing battle with Nasty Newt the pond gangster. It had just got to the bit where Fancy Frog was about to rescue a rather pretty goldfish in distress when a big hairy hand reached out of the back of the television and grabbed Kevin's packet of crisps. The packet disappeared back into the television and Kevin couldn't hear what Fancy Frog was saying for the noise of crunching crisps.

Reggie opened one eye and his

whiskers twitched towards the television like an aerial. His very pleasant dream had been interrupted and he had the strangest feeling that there was another animal in the room. Which was irritating because he would have to get up and growl and curve his back in a menacing sort of way and chase whatever it was down the garden path.

Kevin was annoyed about the crisps — and about missing his programme. It was just his luck to be the only boy in the street with a monster in his television. Then just as he was about to drink his lemonade, the giant hairy hand shot out of the television and grabbed it!

Glug, glug, glug went the television.
Then it burped.

"Mum!" shouted Kevin, really
fed up now. "Mum, there's a
monster in the television and it's
eaten my crisps and drunk my
lemonade!"

"Yes, dear," called Mum from the other room. "Your dad will fix it for you in a minute."

Kevin sighed. Dad had been trying all day to build some shelves in the garage. Every time he put them up they fell down again. Last time Kevin had seen Dad he had a purple face and was jumping up and down on a pile of wooden planks. Not the best time to ask Dad to get rid of a monster in the television. There wasn't likely to be a chapter on it in his DIY book either.

He decided to call his friend Eric.

"Hello, Eric, it's Kevin here. Yes,

I know Fancy Frog's on the telly at the moment, sorry. But I've got a monster in my television. Can you come round and give me a hand?"

When Kevin got back to the living room, Reggie was sitting on the top of the television with his head right down and his nose to the screen, mesmerised.

Fancy Frog had disappeared from the screen and instead there was a huge, horrible, hairy monster face, grinning and chuckling and poking its tongue out at Reggie. Reggie's fur was standing on end and he kept swiping at the face with his paw, but the monster was safely inside the screen.

Then Grandma came in.

"Is the weather on yet, dear?" she asked Kevin.

"No, sorry, Grandma," he answered. "I'm afraid we've got a monster in our television."

"But I always watch the weather!" said Grandma. "Can't you just change the channel?"

They tried, but the hairy monster was on every channel! Grandma decided she'd go next door and watch the weather on their television instead.

"Whatever is the world coming to?" she muttered.

The big hairy hand emerged.from the television again

and grabbed Reggie's tail. Before Kevin could stop him, the monster was swinging poor Reggie around before hurling him onto the sofa, where he landed in a crumpled heap.

The face on the TV screen croaked with glee. Reggie wasn't amused. He picked himself up, put his tail in the air, and with a disdainful sniff over his shoulder, stalked out of the room.

Just then, Eric arrived.

"Have you tried unplugging him?" he suggested helpfully. Kevin hadn't, so they tried. But the big hairy hand just shot out and plugged it in again. It was a real nuisance.

The neighbours came over with Grandma to have a look at the monster. Mr and Mrs Johnson had several suggestions, from making a citizen's arrest to calling the fire brigade. But Kevin's mum thought they might spray water all over her nice new living room carpet.

The word soon spread that there was a monster in the television at number 28. Before long there was a queue outside and Kevin and Eric were organising refreshments and doing a roaring trade in cups of tea and Mum's homemade scones. Dad didn't know what was going on. He was still trying to put up shelves in the garage, but Mum helped Kevin put up a barrier with string around the television. This was after the monster grabbed Mrs Taylor's new hat and ate it in front of her on the screen, giggling as he did so. He even let out a big burp when he'd finished! Mrs Taylor was not impressed.

Two hours later a large van drew up outside and several people got out carrying cameras and microphones.

"Hello!" they shouted, as they marched through the front door, past the waiting neighbours and visitors.

"We're from TVB News. We've come to interview Kevin about the TV monster!"

"How long has this monster been in your television asked the lady reporter in a concerned voice. "Will this change your life? How do you feel?"

"Well, he's been here since Fancy Frog started about a quarter past five," replied Kevin.

"We feel really fed up because that's our favourite programme and it will change our life because

we'll have to go next door to
watch it."

The lady reporter nodded in a
caring sort of way.

"Thank you, Kevin. This is Anna
Badger-Jones at 28 Acacia Avenue,
reporting for TVB."

The next morning, Kevin was
invited onto breakfast television to
talk about his monster. The TV
company came and picked up
Kevin and his television with the
monster inside. In the studio they
plugged the monster in and asked
him questions about the world
situation. All he did was cackle and
croak and try and grab the cameras
with his big hairy hand, but he was

a big hit with the viewers. TVB offered Kevin a brand new television in return for leaving his old television with them. They wanted to give the monster his own regular spot on the breakfast show.

So after that Kevin and Eric were able to watch Fancy Frog every week and enjoy their crisps and lemonade in peace. Now and then, they would turn on the TV

before school and catch *The Mega Monster Show* where the monster had guests like pop stars and government ministers. Even Reggie would sit on the rug and watch, with an occasional twitch of his whiskers.

It was nice to see the monster now and again, but even nicer to be able to turn him off!

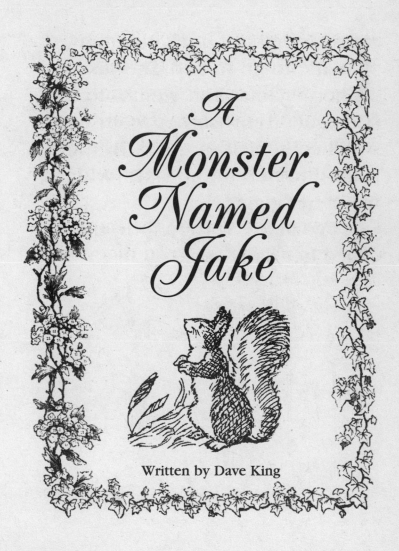

A Monster Named Jake

Written by Dave King

IT WAS eight o'clock, time for Katie to go to bed. She put on her pyjamas and went into the bathroom to brush her teeth. She watched herself in the mirror and started to pull funny faces, which made her giggle.

"What are you up to in there?" called her dad.

"Oh, nothing. Just brushing my teeth," Katie answered.

"Well, hurry up if you want a story," said Dad.

Katie wiped all the froth off her face and ran into her bedroom.

"About time," laughed Dad. "Which story shall we read tonight?"

"Mongo the Monster, please," said Katie.

"Oh, not again. Can't we have a different one?" moaned Dad.

"But it's my favourite," pleaded Katie.

Katie loved monsters. She had lots of monster books and toys and a huge poster of funny looking

monsters on her wall. Katie thought
the biggest one looked like Mongo
in her story book.

Katie snuggled down and
listened to her dad until he finished
the story. As she lay there looking at
her poster, wishing it was real and
she could join the fun, she felt a
little drowsy. She closed her eyes,
and suddenly, she was standing by
one of the trees in the poster and
could hear the monsters talking.

"Has everybody arrived yet?"
she heard Mongo ask, as he
stomped around the forest clearing.

"I think so," answered a little
monster.

Katie watched from behind a

tree as the most amazing monsters appeared. They looked just like the ones she had seen in the story. They were very noisy, stomping about and making the funniest sounds. All the monsters turned to face Mongo.

"Hello, everybody. Welcome to our Monster Competition. I hope

you are all ready for some monster fun! Let's start with our first game. Take your places, everyone, for the Monster Muscle Game."

With that they all cheered and formed a long line behind a huge rock. Katie could not help laughing at them because they were so funny. They wobbled about making strange noises. One of them kept jumping high into the air.

"Boing!" called Mongo. "I know you're excited, but could you stand still for one minute?"

The monsters laughed as Boing turned a deep red.

Katie could not believe her eyes when the first monster lifted the huge rock high above its head and threw it into the air. Within seconds it landed by the tree, narrowly missing Katie's head.

"Help!" she cried.

"What was that? Who's there?" asked Mongo.

"It's me," replied Katie creeping out from where she was hiding.

"Look at that!" bellowed Boing.

"What a funny looking creature," laughed Fang.

"It's all arms and legs," giggled Roly.

"What is it?" asked Boggle.

"What do you mean?" replied Katie. "I'm a little girl, my name is Katie and I don't look half as funny as you!"

"Pleased to meet you," said Mongo. "Where did you come from?"

"Well, I was lying in bed looking at my monster poster, thinking about all the adventures you have when suddenly I found myself in the picture. I was just watching your game when that rock very nearly squashed me," explained Katie.

"I'm glad you like our stories and I'm sorry you nearly got hit, but nobody knew you were there. Why don't you come and join in our games?" suggested Mongo. "I'm sure you'll make an excellent

monster."

"But I couldn't lift that rock, let alone throw it," laughed Katie.

"Well, we can find you one just the right size," said Mongo.

One by one, the monsters threw the rock as hard as they could to see who could throw it the furthest. Last was Katie with a much smaller rock, which she threw with all her might. The monsters cheered. Boing said, "Well done. You're a great monster. You'll love the next game."

All the monsters, including Katie, had to stand in the stickiest mud, and make a set of footprints. Then they each had to guess which set belonged to which monster. It was great fun, but they all got in a terrible mess, which Katie particularly enjoyed.

Next came the roaring game, each monster roaring as loud as it could. "Aaarrrggghhh!" went the first one. "Gggrrraaawww!" went the second. Then it was Katie's turn. "Yaa!" she shouted.

"Louder," giggled Mongo. "You can growl louder than that. Roar right from your toes."

"Ymaaa!" roared Katie, and everyone clapped.

"Well done," shouted Fang.

"Am I making a good monster?" asked Katie.

"One of the best," laughed Fang. "You're a natural."

"What's next?" Katie asked Mongo.

"It's my favourite one. It always makes me laugh till I cry," he said, chuckling. "It's the funny face competition. Each monster stands in front of the others and pulls silly faces."

"No problem. I'm good at pulling faces. I practice all the time at home," she giggled.

"Good. Then again you've got a funny face anyway. You've only got two eyes, one nose and a mouth. That's funny enough," said Mongo, and they both laughed.

They watched as the monsters pulled the most hilarious faces. They all laughed and laughed. But when it was Katie's turn they were all rolling on the ground and holding onto their tummies. They had never seen anything so funny.

After the last game the prizes were given out. Katie won first

prize for the funny face game. Mongo pinned a gold star onto her pyjama jacket. Then they all danced and sang and had a great party.

Suddenly, Katie heard a loud ringing noise and turned to see where it was coming from. It was her alarm clock.

She was lying in bed, all twisted up in her duvet.

"Oh! I don't want to be back here. I was enjoying my monster adventure," she said to herself. As she untangled herself from her duvet she let out a cry. "Ouch!" She had pricked her finger on something sharp. She looked down at her pyjama jacket and saw the small gold star. "Oh wow! Then it wasn't just a dream!" Katie jumped out of bed and went over to her poster.

All the monsters were there as before, as well as a small girl behind a tree.

"It's me!" Katie gasped. She thought she saw Mongo wink.

"Thank you. I had a lovely time. It'll be our secret," she whispered. Just then Katie's mum came in to say good morning.

"Hello, Katie. Sleep well?" asked Mum.

"The best ever," replied Katie. Mum looked down and saw mud all over Katie's feet.

"Look at your feet! They're filthy! Go and wash them at once. Whatever have you been doing?" asked Mum.

"Just dreaming," replied Katie, as she winked at Mongo.

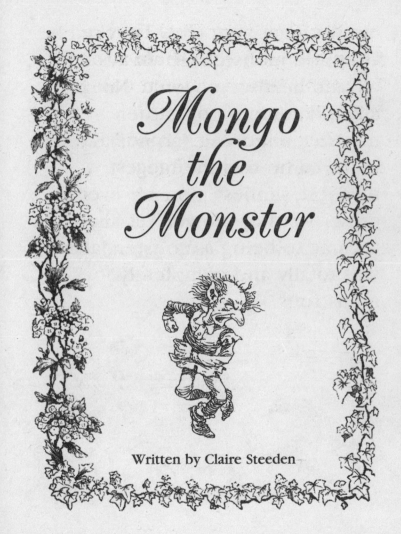

Mongo the Monster

Written by Claire Steeden

JAKE KEGWORTH truly believed he was a monster. He always had and he always would. Not just any old common or garden monster, mind you. Oh no, Jake believed he was the biggest, meanest, slimiest monster ever to growl, snarl or glower. Yes sir, when it came to being a monster, Jake was totally and completely monstrous.

Of course, there were certain monster-type things that he was unable to do. He wasn't allowed to eat his younger brother, Michael, for instance. He had thought about it once or twice (usually in the middle of the night, when eighteen-month-old Michael — with whom Jake shared a bedroom — was crying for attention or food, or whatever it was baby brothers cried for at such unsociable hours). But Jake's mother had made it quite clear to him that even the meanest of monsters did not eat their younger brothers, nor any member of the family for that matter.

Neither was Jake able to leave

slime trails in his wake. This was a particularly sore point with him, as Jake believed this to be the most basic of monster habits. But once again, Jake's mother was adamant!

"There are to be no slime trails left around our nicely decorated house!" she would say, before looking skywards with that peculiar kind of look that only exasperated mothers can give. And naturally, Jake's complete lack of slimy tentacles, along with his quite normal amount of eyes, arms, legs and so on, did put something of a damper on his efforts to scare the living daylights out of Mrs Ricklesworth, his elderly next door neighbour. Jake was, of course, a young monster, so his view of Mrs Ricklesworth's age was not quite accurate. In everybody else's eyes — including her own — she was in her late forties.) No matter how often he waved his arms about, or writhed and wriggled his fingers in what Jake felt was a distinctly creepy manner, Mrs Ricklesworth remained quite unnervingly cool.

"Ah!" Jake thought, in his darkest moments. "But if I had even

one purple tentacle, things would be very different. Oh yes! "

Despite all this, Jake still believe-ed himself to be much better at being a monster than anybody else he knew — although he would occasionally and grudg-ingly admit to himself that Mr Pink, the mathematics teacher at Jake's school was not too far behind him in the monster stakes, even if he did have a silly name for a monster!

Now although Jake believed himself to be a monster, few other people took him at his word. Can you believe that? Despite all the evidence Jake had at his disposal, when he referred to himself as a monster his friends would just laugh and say:

"If you're really a monster, Jake, where are all your monster friends?"

So it was that one morning, Jake decided to put all doubts of his monster-hood to rest.

He went to the *Yellow Pages* and scoured the listings, he looked for Monster Taxis and Monster Dry Cleaners and even Monsters For Hire, but he couldn't find a hint of anything even vaguely connected to monsters!

His friends, watching from outside the window, were most

curious to know why Jake was looking so intently through the phone book.

"Perhaps he's going mad?" one of them suggested.

They were even more bewildered when Jake let out a yelp of delight and began jumping around the room in a most peculiar manner. They watched as he dashed to the telephone and made a call. When Jake had finished, one of his friends tapped on the window. Jake rushed over, threw the window open and declared,

"You are all invited to tea on Saturday, when I shall prove to you once and for all that I'm a monster!"

Naturally enough, word spread around the town that something was going to be happening on Saturday and everyone became excited at the thought of Jake making a very large fool of himself.

"Perhaps this will finally free the poor boy from the crazy idea that he is a monster! It would make my life a lot more peaceful, I can tell you!" Mrs Ricklesworth said to her good friend, Mrs Parker (about whom we shall perhaps talk some other time, when you will learn of the fate that befell her husband during an attempt to cross the English Channel on a raft made of sponge-cake).

Saturday came (as Saturdays do) and brought with it a large crowd of interested onlookers gathering around the Kegworth household. The crowd became more and more excited as the afternoon wore on, calling for proof of Jake's monster status. In fact, they became so loud that Jake's poor mother developed the most frightful headache!

Jake's friends arrived for tea at five minutes before four o'clock, each of them looking a little nervous, if truth be told (and of course, it is). And at four o'clock precisely, everyone, including Mrs Ricklesworth, Jake's family and friends and all of the interested onlookers, fell into a hushed silence. What was about to happen? What was Jake about to do?

By five minutes after four, the crowd was getting restless, and murmurs of "I told you so," could be heard. Nothing had happened, of course!

How silly of them to think that something would. Poor Jake was beginning to look a little green (which is something that all good monsters know how to do, by the way).

Just then, a large, brightly painted coach drew up outside the house.

And what do you think happened? Well, I'll tell you ... the coach doors opened and out walked the most revolting bunch of monsters you've never wanted to see (or perhaps you have, in which case you may well be a monster, too!)

They were slimy, nasty, icky and yucky looking, with all kinds of tentacles, claws, eyes on stalks, lumps and bumps. It's fairly safe to say, that they were an unbelievably ugly bunch, even by monster standards, and they are pretty low!

They made their way up the garden path and Jake opened the front door

"Hello, my friends!" he said. "How nice to meet you all at last! Do come in and have some tea!"

"Hello, Jake!" said the biggest monster, through at least sixteen mouths. "I hope you've got some chocolate biscuits, because as you probably know, monsters simply adore chocolate biscuits!"

Sure enough, Jake had chocolate biscuits, along with all kinds of other nice things to eat.

They all sat down to tea, and neither Jake's family, his friends or the rest of the town, ever doubted again that Jake was a true monster! After all, who else but a monster would invite other monsters to tea?

Now you might be wondering how Jake eventually contacted the other monsters? It was really very simple, he looked in the phone book under "Clubs and Associations" and found the number for the "Monster Society and Social Club". If you'd like, you can give them a call and invite some monsters round for tea, but you'd probably best check with your mother first, because as Jake's mother found, monsters really do leave slime trails everywhere they go!